THE WORLD OF
LETITIA ELIZABETH LANDON

*A Literary Celebrity
of the 1830s*

Yours obliged
L. E. Landon

AUTHOR OF "ROMANCE AND REALITY".

L. E. L. (CAT. 58)

THE WORLD OF
LETITIA ELIZABETH LANDON

A Literary Celebrity of the 1830s

EXHIBITION AT THE GROLIER CLUB

BY

F. J. SYPHER

NEW YORK

The Grolier Club

2011

EXHIBITION:

Wednesday, March 23, 2011 through Friday, May 27, 2011

Members' Gallery

THE GROLIER CLUB

47 East 60th Street, New York, NY 10022

ISBN 978-1-60583-031-5

CONTENTS

ACKNOWLEDGEMENTS

THANKS ARE DUE to the Grolier Club for sponsoring and mounting this exhibition, and specifically to a number of people at the Grolier Club for much-appreciated advice: Mary and Bruce Crawford, Eric Holzenberg, Anne Hoy, Jerry Kelly, George Ong, Mark Samuels Lasner, Megan Smith, Szilvia Szmuk-Tanenbaum, the late Charles J. Tanenbaum, the members of the Committee on Members' Exhibitions, and others. Individuals and organizations that provided digital photographic files for use in this exhibition and catalogue are gratefully acknowledged with credit lines in the relevant catalogue entries. Thanks also to many others, and especially to Gillian Gear for information on maps of East Barnet; to Sue Matoff for correspondence about Jerdan; and to Julie Watt for photos taken in Aberford.

JUNE 30, 2010   *F. J. Sypher*

THE WORLD OF
LETITIA ELIZABETH LANDON

A Literary Celebrity of the 1830s

LETITIA ELIZABETH LANDON (or "L. E. L." as she signed her work) was an international literary celebrity in her day—admired for her wit and brilliant personality, and as the prolific author of seventeen volumes of poems; three three-volume novels; two collections of short stories; a drama; essays; hundreds of uncollected poems contributed to periodicals, gift books, anthologies, and other volumes; not to mention many anonymous reviews, articles, and critical essays published in periodicals. Her first publication appeared in a magazine on March 11, 1820, a few months before her eighteenth birthday, and her first book came out in the summer of 1821. She died suddenly in 1838, in West Africa, where she had gone as the wife of a colonial official, George Maclean.

During her too-brief lifetime, Landon frequented prominent literary salons in London and Paris, and her work was distributed in major capitals from Paris to St. Petersburg; translated into French, German, and Dutch; and reviewed in Continental literary journals. Editions of her poems and novels appeared in Boston, New York, and Philadelphia, and were reviewed and discussed in American magazines and newspapers. After her death, her collected poems remained in print in Britain and in the United States until the 1890s; since 1990 they have again become available, together with reprints of her novels, stories, critical writings, letters, and uncollected poems.

Why then, is Landon not better known? For one thing, she wrote much of her most important work in the 1830s, a period that has been cast into the shadow because it was preceded by great Romantics such as Scott, Byron, Shelley, and Keats; and followed by great Victorians such as Tennyson, Browning, Thackeray, and Dickens. Also, Landon wrote in a manner that was frankly sentimental; her typical themes are "Sorrow, Beauty, Love and Death."[1] Such writing went out of fashion as later readers demanded works dealing with social, political, religious, and philosophic issues. In addition, Landon was closely associated with the literary annuals—a publishing phenomenon of the 1820s and 1830s. By about 1840 the British annuals were mostly defunct, and Landon's work came to be associated with the passé fashions of another era.

But Landon has never been forgotten. Even after her works went out of print in the 1890s, she continued to be a subject of interest in the twentieth century because of continuing fascination with her personal history, especially her death in West Africa.[2] Since the 1980s Landon has drawn increasing attention for her achievement as a single woman carving out a successful literary career in the tough arena of literary London.

Many of her contemporary readers imagined Landon to live in glamorous sur-roundings, and write in a luxurious, romantic study lined with rose-colored silk, but the reality was that she lived for most of her adult life in a tiny, crudely-furnished attic room at a London boarding house. She moved in fashionable circles, and her books were published in expensive editions, but she lived entirely on what she earned from her writing, while making substantial contributions to the support of members of her family. These are some of the striking contradictions that make Landon's life a fasci-nating study, apart from the literary works that continue to carry her distinctive voice.

Contemporaries such as Bulwer (later, Bulwer Lytton), Thackeray, Landor, Whittier, and Poe admired Landon's work. Readers appreciated her lyric gift as shown in short poems perfect in their rendering of fleeting moods and delicate observations. Her longer poems abound in rich imagery, and powerfully expressed feeling. Her novels of contem-porary life, *Romance and Reality* (1831) and *Lady Anne Granard* (1842), present lively social satire and sharp aphorisms, while her historical novels, especially *Ethel Churchill* (1837), offer powerful character analysis, as well as vivid portraits of society. Landon's acute critical faculties and gifts of wit and observation are everywhere apparent in her critical writings and in her letters.

I. EARLY YEARS

ACCORDING to the record of her baptism, Landon was born on August 14, 1802.[3] The Landon family roots (cat. 1) were in Herefordshire, where her father John Landon (baptized in 1756) had grown up as the eldest son of John Landon (1722–1782), rector of the rural parish of Tedstone Delamere. Two brothers of the younger John Landon made their careers in the Church: James Landon (cat. 2), a fellow of Oriel College, Oxford, was vicar of Aberford, Yorkshire; Whittington Landon (cat. 3), a graduate of Worcester College, Oxford, became provost of the college, and concurrently dean of Exeter Cathedral. However, John Landon went to sea, and as a midshipman voyaged to southern Africa and to Jamaica.[4] He later settled in London, and in 1795 joined a partnership of army agents—bankers for military accounts. During the French wars this was a flourishing and highly profitable line of business.

Having established himself in his new career, John Landon married Catherine Jane

Bishop, June 15, 1797, at the Church of St. Luke, Chelsea. About all that is presently known of her earlier history and antecedents is that she was born in France circa 1770–1772, a British subject, the daughter of Mrs. Letitia Bishop (1749/50–1832), who later lived in Sloane Street on a private income from some undetermined source. There are no indications of who Mr. Bishop might have been, or even if such a person ever existed. In fact, it might be well to point out right now that there is considerable uncertainty about many substantive matters relating to Letitia Landon and her family. The memoirs about her were written by people with little or no intimate knowledge of her background, and there is no known collection of family papers that could shed light on important unanswered questions.[5]

According to the standard memoirs, the family at the time of Landon's birth was living in a Georgian town house at 25 Hans Place (cat. 4). They were parishioners of the Church of St. Luke, known as Chelsea Old Church (cat. 5), where Landon was baptized on October 18th, 1805, as recorded in the church register. This is the earliest documentary record about her. Her brother, Whittington Henry Landon, was also baptized at St. Luke's. In addition there seems to have been a younger sister, Elizabeth Jane Landon, who died of consumption at the age of about thirteen. Letitia Landon as a small child in London is said to have attended classes at Miss Rowden's school, which has gained a certain fame from alumnae such as Caroline Lamb, and Mary Russell Mitford.

This was the period of the Napoleonic wars, and prices of farm produce rose to

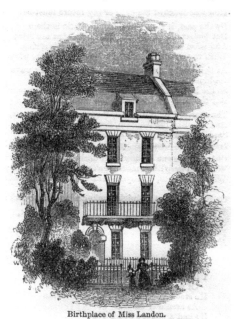

Birthplace of Miss Landon.

25 Hans Place (CAT. 4)

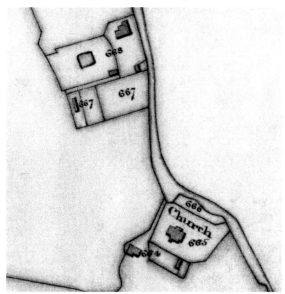

Trevor Park and the Church of St. Mary the Virgin, East Barnet, 1818 (CAT. 6, *enlarged detail; courtesy Hertfordshire Archives & Local Studies*) – *house near top, with square pond left*

Church of St. Mary the Virgin, East Barnet, 1817 (CAT. 7)

Church of St. Mary the Virgin, East Barnet, 1807 (CAT. 8)

WATER END HOUSE.

Water End House (CAT. 9) – *contemporary with, and of similar proportions to Trevor Park, of which no view is known*

record highs. Landon's father invested in a 216-acre property known as Coventry Farm (now Mill Hill Golf Club) in the parish of Hendon, in the environs of London. About 1809, the family took up residence at East Barnet, in a historic country house known as Trevor Park (cat. 6, 9), dating from 1611, with about twenty-seven acres of grounds adjacent to the ancient Church of St. Mary the Virgin (cat. 7, 8) with its picturesque churchyard. Landon states in her brief untitled autobiographical account, written in 1837 for *The Book of Gems,* that her childhood was passed at Trevor Park; she says nothing to indicate that she had previously lived in London, although in one of her letters she expresses her belief that she was born in Chelsea.[6] At Trevor Park she loved wandering about in the old overgrown gardens and woods; her favorite haunt was a shady pond with a little island where she would go to read and imagine herself as a modern-day Robinson Crusoe.

During these years the future poet was educated at home, principally by her cousin Elizabeth Landon, whose instruction was supplemented with lessons from tutors in French, writing, and music. Serious reading included Rollin's *Ancient History,* Hume's

History of England, Plutarch's *Lives,* and other standard works. Letitia Landon also delighted in the poems of Sir Walter Scott (cat. 10). Favorite books, given to Landon by her father, included an edition of the *Arabian Nights,* and a copy of *Sylvester Tramper* (cat. 11), a tale of African adventures. She and her brother read extensively from volumes of poets and novelists in Cooke's Pocket Library (cat. 12), a popular series that also fed the early imaginations of Hazlitt, Dickens, and Leigh Hunt. Landon began to compose poetry as a young child, and recalled reciting her verses to herself while lying awake at night. She is said to have begun writing them down almost as soon as she learned how to trace letters on a slate.

II. LITERARY BEGINNINGS

THE END of the Napoleonic wars in 1815 brought Britain both peace and economic depression. With the demobilization of forces John Landon's army agency declined; at the same time, the price of agricultural produce fell drastically. He gave up Coventry Farm and Trevor Park, and in 1817 the family moved to Old Brompton (cat. 13), where—as luck or fate would have it—across the lane lived William Jerdan (cat. 14, 15), editor of *The Literary Gazette,* a popular and influential weekly journal (cat. 16). In his *Autobiography* he recalled: "My first recollection of the future poetess is that of a plump girl, grown enough to be almost mistaken for a woman, bowling a hoop round the walks, with a hoop-stick in one hand, and a book in the other, reading as she ran, and as well as she could manage both exercise and instruction at the same time. The exercise was prescribed and insisted upon: the book was her own irrepressible choice."[7]

Brompton Villa (CAT. 13)

Early in 1820 Landon's mother, thinking that her daughter's literary talent might be enlisted to help the family finances, urged her tutor to write to their neighbor to ask his opinion of some of Letitia Landon's verses. On receiving a favorable reply Mrs. Landon expressed the hope that there might be room for some lines in a forthcoming issue of *The Literary Gazette.* Jerdan obliged

L. E. L. (CAT. 29)

William Jerdan (CAT. 14)

by including in the number for Saturday, March 11, 1820 Landon's short poem titled "Rome"—her first publication, signed simply "L." Others soon followed, and plans were made to publish a book.

During the summer of 1820 Landon worked on her narrative poem "The Fate of Adelaide," the main piece of her projected volume, during her visit to friends and relatives at Clifton, and at Castle End, at Lea (near Ross-on-Wye), then in Gloucestershire, now Herefordshire. At this time her family gave up the lease on their house, Brompton Villa, which in July was offered at auction "for immediate occupancy."[8] There are no available indications of where the Landons moved, and it seems possible that at this time the family broke up, as suggested by Anna Maria Hall in her novel *A Woman's Story* (1857), based to some extent on Landon's life. Relatively little is known about Letitia Landon's activities from 1820 until 1824 except that she continued to publish in the *Gazette,* and (to judge from her letters) she was living in London.

The Fate of Adelaide, a Swiss Romantic Tale; and Other Poems (cat. 17) appeared in the summer of 1821 with a dedication to Sarah Siddons (cat. 18), a famous stage personality, and a friend of Landon's grandmother. A polite notice appeared in *The Literary Gazette,* and a brief mention in *The New Monthly Magazine.* But the publisher, John Warren, of Bond Street, went out of business, and Landon never collected any of the profits owed her.

From September 1821, when she began publishing poetical sketches in *The Literary Gazette* under the tantalizing signature "L. E. L.," Landon began to attract an enthusiastic following among readers. Edward Bulwer, then an undergraduate at Cambridge, remembered:

> At that time, poetry was not yet out of fashion, at least with us of the cloister; and there was always, in the Reading Room of the Union, a rush every Saturday afternoon for "The Literary Gazette," and an impatient anxiety to hasten at once to that corner of the sheet which contained the three magical letters of "L. E. L." And all of us praised the verse, and all of us guessed at the author. We soon learned it was a female, and our admiration was doubled, and our conjectures tripled. Was she young? Was she pretty? and—for there were some embryo fortune hunters among us—was she rich?[9]

The enigmatic palindromic initials attracted wider notice after Jerdan in February 1822 announced in the journal the remarkable fact that the talented author was a "lady, yet in her teens!" (Jerdan's exclamation point).[10] All through 1822 and 1823, hardly a week went by without one or more compositions by L. E. L. appearing in *The Literary Gazette*. In addition to sentimental sketches, she published graceful, elegant lyrics, and soon began also contributing unsigned articles and reviews of books, art shows, and theatrical peformances.

Landon contributed two poems to *Forget Me Not*, published by Rudolph Ackermann late in 1823, for the year 1824 (cat. 25), the second issue of the attractive little book that initiated the British vogue for literary annuals. In 1824 she wrote three songs for John Howard Payne's successful drama *Charles the Second; or, the Merry Monarch*, presented with music by Henry R. Bishop (cat. 19, 20), a well-known composer then, remembered today for his song "Home, Sweet Home." Her lyrics were highly popular for setting to music (cat. 48); there is record of nearly 100 songs written to poems by Landon.[11]

III. A BEST-SELLER OF 1824

LANDON'S most popular work, *The Improvisatrice* (cat. 21), came out in July 1824 but it had actually been written about a year earlier, and had made the rounds of several publishers before being accepted by Hurst, Robinson and Co., London agents of the firm of Archibald Constable (cat. 22), Walter Scott's publisher in Edinburgh. At this time Landon was living with her grandmother in an apartment at 131 Sloane Street.

The Improvisatrice was an instant best-seller, with nearly the entire edition bought up on the first day of publication. A second edition appeared in September, and a third before the end of the year. Three more editions came out in 1825, as well as an American edition, published in Boston, and a seventh edition appeared in 1826.

The unusual title alludes to the heroine of Madame de Staël's *Corinne ou l'Italie* (1807), a book that profoundly influenced Landon and her contemporaries by its moving depiction of a gifted young woman's literary career in Italy. Like Corinne, Landon's Florentine heroine composes inspired verse by improvisation, and is involved in a beautiful but unhappy love affair that ends with her death. Her lover, Lorenzo, secludes himself for a lifetime of mourning and regret. The special appeal of Landon's poem lay in its lush, highly-charged—one might almost say erotic, certainly sensual—imagery.

The Improvisatrice was discussed sympathetically in leading magazines, but Jerdan in his review for *The Literary Gazette* went overboard with praise, pronouncing such absurdities as "we can adduce no instance, ancient or modern, of similar talent and excellence."[12] Obviously he was trying to further his protégée's career. But reviewers ridiculed Jerdan's outrageous puffery, and warned Landon not to take it too seriously. Jerdan's fulsome reviews of her work may in the long run have done Landon almost as much harm as good.

Landon's success brought her to the attention of Alaric A. Watts (cat. 26), editor of a new literary annual titled *The Literary Souvenir* (cat. 27), where she became a regular contributor. He corresponded with her about her plans for her next volume, *The Troubadour* (cat. 28), composed along similar lines to *The Improvisatrice*. In the conclusion, the heroine, Eva, is mistress of a tournament of song, won by her lover Raymond.

While Landon was working on her new book, her father died. As mentioned earlier, little is known about the Landon family after they left Brompton Villa in 1820. Records of the Court of Chancery show that John Landon had previously been involved in legal disputes with his partners over monies handled by the army agency, and that he admitted that he had received more than his share. One infers that he was unable to pay back what he owed, and that his finances then went into irretrievable difficulties.

Alaric A. Watts (CAT. 26)

Exactly what form these difficulties took remains to be determined, most likely through research in court papers. He evidently fell into such miserable (or, in the view of the time, shameful) circumstances that none of Landon's contemporary memoirists even hints at what happened.[13] The silence is so complete that there is not even an indication of where or when he died; the burial register of the remote rural parish of Yarpole, Herefordshire, where his brother Whittington Landon was the absentee rector, attests that John Landon was buried there on November 18, 1824. No death notice or obituary has been located. The devastating emotional effect upon Letitia Landon is apparent in one of the most moving passages in *The Troubadour*, a concluding elegy on her father.

The Troubadour, published in July 1825, became another commercial and critical success, and went rapidly through three large editions. An American edition was published in Philadelphia; and the book circulated on the Continent, where it was reviewed in the Paris journal *Le Globe*, and available in Germany, as indicated by an inscribed copy given to Goethe's daughter-in-law as a "present" from her mother: "Ottilie von Goethe. Geschenk der Mutter."[14]

Toward the end of 1825 Landon and her publisher Archibald Constable traveled north from London in a private carriage. Landon was going to Aberford—a coaching stop about halfway between London and Edinburgh—to visit her uncle James Landon, while Constable proceeded to his home at Lasswade, Scotland. On the trip with them was Richard Milliken, who kept a diary, published anonymously in 1902. It seems never to have been cited in connection with Landon before now, and it gives a most interesting record of her conversation and of the impression that she made. The first entry is dated November 4, 1825:

> Before leaving home I had a great wish to meet L. E. L. in London, and made many inquiries as to the possibility; yet chances seemed against me. But the same Being who generally accomplishes my lawful wishes brought about this also; for I am now travelling with the said L. E. L. in a private carriage on her way to York, in charge of A. Constable, and eagerly caught every blossom of wit as it budded from her flowery imagination. She thinks that "Love is predestined," that it is the "scarlet-fever of the Heart," yet positively declares that she never felt the bitter arrows. L. E. L. believes there are such non-describables as "ghosts"; indeed, Constable told an anecdote which occurred to himself (evidently proving himself a true believer). This was that previous to his second marriage a figure appeared by the bedside, a fine handsome female very like the present wife. Good figure; but he is a Scotsman. L. E. L. expresses a regard for Dr Maginn, who, she says, has addressed some lines to her eyebrows. [*Here follows a brief editorial identification of Maginn.*]

5th November.—Set out this morning at six. Talked very freely with L. E. L., finding fault with her mode of life, guarding her against her literary friends' free opinions of Religion. She said she could not believe that I was so sincere as I professed to be; abuses the idea of platonic love, yet she professes the greatest friendship for Mr Jerdan (friendship is platonic love when between the sexes); her friendship is built upon gratitude. Mr J. it is who has always been her best friend. "Gratitude is the memory of the Heart." Thus we find it rise from a pure source, and so continue its course until it arrives at what is called Platonic love. Would not L. E. L. be much annoyed if I told her that her friendship was perhaps mixed with the passion? Will not marry a medical man; will wait for me five years (she may wait fifty); will not have a man who sings or plays. Dreads death, yet wishes to be dissected; had an uncle who was buried alive—fears the same. Is an orphan; never went to school; is supported by her grandmother; her connections very good; is going on a visit to her uncle, Rev. Mr Landon, Rector, Abbeyfield, near York. We exchanged cards; promised to send her Wolfe's *Remains;* repeated the first verse of my parody on his beautiful lines, at which she laughed heartily; her conversation very like her writings, airy and trifling, "Writings upon the lines of a Rainbow," &c. We left her at her uncle's this evening; had to walk through a churchyard; she felt quite agitated. She is not handsome—no sweetness of expression; has read very little; some French.[15]

In later years Landon gave wide scope to her talents as she branched out into fields of fiction, criticism, and drama. But at this point in her career it can be said that she had arrived on the international scene as a new and brilliant star.

IV. *LEO OF SALONS*

THE SUCCESS of *The Improvisatrice* and *The Troubadour* opened doors for Landon as a *leo* ("lion") in literary salons. In August 1824 she was corresponding with Elizabeth Isabella Spence, who conducted a salon where writers, especially women writers, could meet to discuss literary matters. At these events Landon encountered such literary figures as Elizabeth Ogilvy Benger (cat. 30), Lady Caroline Lamb, Rosina Wheeler (later Lady Lytton) (cat. 34), Katherine Thomson, Emma Roberts, and Samuel Carter Hall (cat. 32), through whom Landon met Anna Maria Hall (cat. 31), who was to become one of her closest friends. Few of these names are familiar today, but they were active figures on the contemporary literary scene, and several became valuable contacts for Landon throughout her professional life.

At 22 Hans Place, conducted by the Lance sisters as a day school and boarding house for women, where Landon lived from late 1826, she seems to have established a salon of her own. After hours she was able to use the schoolroom for receptions and even for dance parties, like the fancy-dress ball that she and her friend Emma Roberts gave in 1827. Frances Trollope wrote: "It was really a very smart party, though *some of us* did look rather queer."[16] Landon's fondness for somewhat flamboyant costume is suggested in a portrait done at about this time by William Pickersgill (cat. 29). A portrait by Adam Buck, reproduced in an anthology published in 1826, was said to be so unlike her as to be utterly unrecognizeable (cat. 36).

Among other influential literary acquaintances during this period was Edward Bulwer (cat. 35), who married Rosina Wheeler (cat. 34) in 1827. Landon was frequently their guest, as at Woodcot, the handsome country house where they lived

Rosina Lytton, née Wheeler (CAT. 34)

when first married. She also became friendly—some thought too friendly—with the brilliant journalist William Maginn (cat. 33), who was a leading spirit of *Fraser's Magazine,* and whose association with Landon was later the subject of damaging rumor. And she remained close to her mentor William Jerdan.

Her relationship with Jerdan was and remains a conspicuous topic of comment and speculation. Jerdan, born in 1782, was twenty years older than Landon; he had been married since 1806 and had seven children. He later wrote that Landon had been so enthusiastic in her gratitude to him for furthering her literary ambitions that she constructed around him an intense fantasy attachment that infused all her early poems with imaginary passion.[17] But some thought at the time that their attachment was not based on fantasy, but was a real love affair.

Rumors surfaced in London newspapers with leering accounts of her and Jerdan as lovers. An article published in March 1826 said that in September 1825 she had been caught *flagrante delicto* with Jerdan at his house while his wife and children were at the seashore, and that Landon had previously given birth to a child fathered by him.[18] In September 1826 another paper rumored that she had been pregnant earlier in the year, and had gone off to the country to have the baby during the summer, and had lately appeared back in town "as thin and aereal as ever."[19]

On the other hand, to judge from Landon's correspondence she traveled to visit her relatives in Yorkshire in June 1826, remained there through the summer, then stayed with friends at Biggleswade, Bedfordshire (on the north-south coaching route), and did not arrive back in London until late December, when she took up residence at 22 Hans Place (cat. 37, 38). In later years a cousin, the Reverend James T. B. Landon, stated that the rumor had never been of concern within her family, since Landon had been with them during the time when she was said to have been pregnant.[20]

Memoirists such as Anna Maria Hall, and Katherine Thomson (married to Landon's personal physician, A. T. Thomson), who were close friends of Landon's, are unanimous in their denial of the scandal, and imply that they and others who saw her regularly—both during this period and all through the years would have been well aware if Landon had been pregnant. But the rumors persisted throughout her career. Anonymous letters were sent to her and others, with accusations of illicit affairs, children, and unspecified "criminalities."[21] The rumors were believed by many and did considerable damage to her reputation. The issue remains a lively topic of discussion today, and indications have recently been presented to show that Landon had three children by Jerdan.[22] But there still remain open questions, and the matter has not yet been conclusively decided.

No. 22 Hans Place,

22 Hans Place (CAT. 37)

Attic, 22 Hans Place (CAT. 38)

V. VISITS TO YORKSHIRE

LANDON'S UNCLE in Yorkshire, the Reverend James Landon, vicar of the Church of St. Ricarius (cat. 42), at Aberford, had a large, cheerful, hospitable family. He and his wife Anne Bainbridge had eight children born between 1809 and 1826, seven girls and one boy; in 1827 another girl, Isabella, was born (she lived until 1911). Landon in one of her letters describes the vicarage as a sizeable structure (cat. 41) with bewildering hallways and stairs.[23]

Over the years Landon paid many visits to Aberford, both in the summer and at Christmas-time. While there she took the opportunity to travel in the area, as for example to Leeds, and into Scotland, where she visited Kilchurn Castle (cat. 43). In her poem "Follow Me" she quotes in her title the motto on the Campbell family arms sculpted in relief over the entrance to the castle, and offers ironic commentary on the remaining ruins.

About the time of Landon's return to London in late December 1826, her third important volume of poems appeared, *The Golden Violet* (cat. 39), dedicated "To the Rev. James Landon" at Aberford, where she had been working on the contents during the summer before. Her previous publisher, Hurst, Robinson and Co., had collapsed in the financial debacle surrounding Constable and Sir Walter Scott, and rights to Landon's works had been transferred to Longman, who brought out the volume. He also reprinted or reissued *The Improvisatrice* and *The Troubadour,* and with *The Golden Violet* distributed the books as a three-volume set with collective title-pages headed *The Poetical Works of L. E. L.: A New Edition* (1827).

The Golden Violet continues the themes of *The Troubadour* with another contest of song in a courtly medieval setting. Also in the volume is "Erinna," a poetic account of Landon's literary career. The book was well received, but it did not go into a second edition at this time.

Landon's *The Venetian Bracelet* (cat. 40)

The Rev. James Landon (CAT. 2; *courtesy the Rev. Bernard H. Fray, Priest-in-Charge of Aberford and Micklefield; photo by Paul Watt)*

*Vicarage, Aberford, pre-1861 (*CAT. 41; *courtesy the Rev. Bernard H. Fray, Priest-in-Charge of Aberford and Micklefield; photo by Paul Watt) – church door is visible at right*

*Church of St. Ricarius, Aberford, pre-1861 (*CAT. 42; *courtesy the Rev. Bernard H. Fray, Priest-in-Charge of Aberford and Micklefield; photo by Paul Watt) – vicarage is out of view left; note figures in walk (C. P. Eden, vicar 1850–1885)*

appeared in 1829 and was widely reviewed, but sold weakly. From 1829 Longman issued Landon's *Poetical Works* with *The Venetian Bracelet* as a fourth volume. But by the late 1820s poetry was generally "out," and fiction was "in." Landon decided to try her hand at a three-volume novel.

VI. THE NOVELIST

LANDON'S *Romance and Reality,* 3 vols. (Colburn and Bentley, 1831) (cat. 44, 45), a novel of contemporary society, belongs to the "silver-fork" school of fiction, exemplified by Bulwer's *Pelham* (1828). Landon includes thinly-disguised sketches of Edward and Rosina Bulwer, Anna Maria Hall, and many other literary contemporaries. The main interest is in the scenes and vignettes, and in the witty *bons mots* of chit-chat at parties. A Berlin literary journal, *Magazin für die Literatur des Auslandes,* in 1832 noticed Landon's *Romance and Reality* (translating the title as *Roman und Wirklichkeit*), and gave eighteen quotations (in German translation) to illustrate the author's aphoristic wit.[24] English reviewers such as Landon's friend Maria Jane Jewsbury commented on the artificial and unconvincing plot, but admired the scenes.[25] Bulwer in his review also noted shortcomings, but overall praised the book warmly. In general, reviewers congratulated Landon on taking the leap from poetry to fiction; from a *wunderkind* she was becoming a mature and versatile author.

The novel was immediately reprinted in New York by Harper and Brothers, 2 vols. (1832), and in 1838 republished in an American edition of Landon's *Works,* which brought together both her poetry and fiction (this 1048-page publication went through many reprints until at least 1860). A Dutch translation appeared, *Waarheid en verdichting: een verhaal,* 5 vols. (Zalt-Bommel, 1848). And in 1848 the London publisher Richard Bentley brought out *Romance and Reality* as No. CXI (reprinted 1852) in his series of Standard Novels, with an engraved frontispiece illustration. This title was reissued in 1856 by Ward and Lock with a colored pictorial cover (2s.), and in cloth (2/6). In 1858 the work was purchased by James Blackwood, and issued in 1859 (5th thousand) in a two-shilling edition with an illustrated cover.[26] Blackwood in July 1871 brought out a cloth-bound edition (5s.) with eight full-page engraved illustrations by John Gilbert. Although *Romance and Reality* may not have been the critics' choice of Landon's several novels, it was clearly the most popular.

At about this time Landon also published short stories in annuals and magazines. Some of these are of remarkably high quality for their vivid characterizations and settings, such as the stories in *Heath's Book of Beauty* for 1833 (cat. 47), for which she wrote the entire contents. But reviewers regarded annuals as decorative publications, and did not normally pay serious attention to their literary content. For a writer of fiction to gain a reputation at this time, it was essential to bring out successful three-decker novels.

Landon's next effort in this genre, *Francesca Carrara,* was published by Bentley (cat. 78) in three volumes in 1834. It is a historical novel, and begins in Landon's beloved Italy, but soon the action moves to the court of Louis XIV, and then to England in the aftermath of the Civil War. Reviewers saw *Francesca Carrara* as a significant advance for Landon as a novelist. The book appeared in German translation by C. W. Geisler, 3 vols. (Bremen, 1835). Several editions appeared in the United States, and Routledge later included it as No. 228 in the Railway Library series (1862).

Encouraged by this success, Landon turned again to historical material in *Ethel Churchill; or, the Two Brides,* published in three volumes by Henry Colburn in 1837. She sets the story in a slightly later period, and once more mixes fictional characters with historical figures, such as Pope, and Robert Walpole. Critics have been virtually unanimous in regarding this as Landon's best novel and one of her finest works. The complex plot is skillfully managed, and the characters show real depth. Furthermore, most of the 116 chapters have original verse headings which are among Landon's finest poetic compositions.

Ethel Churchill was published and reprinted in the United States; issued in Germany in a translation by Karl Leon von Soltau, *Adele Churchill, oder die zwei Bräute,* 3 vols. (Leipzig, 1839); and translated into Dutch as *Ethel Churchill, of de twee bruiden,* 3 vols. (Middleburg, 1844). In 1857 a somewhat abridged English version was published in Hodgson's Parlour Library series.

At the time of her death in 1838 Landon was at work on an engaging novel of contemporary society, *Lady Anne Granard; or, Keeping up Appearances.* It was eventually completed by an unidentified (but skilful and talented) author, and published in three volumes by Colburn in 1842, and an abridged version was brought out by Hodgson in 1857.

Landon "edited" (as stated on the otherwise anonymous title-page) a novel titled *Duty and Inclination,* published by Colburn in three volumes in 1838; but all indications are that she did not write the book, which has been attributed to Mme. de Gaudrion. The story is completely lacking in the reflective and philosophical passages that are so characteristic of Landon's fiction. The characters are conventional, the dialogue pedestrian, and the plot filled with clichés. The reviewer for *The Literary Gazette* seems justified in concluding: "A more tedious, trashy, and uninteresting novel, it has seldom been our ill-luck to have to wade through."[27] However, there is an interesting preface by Landon, mentioning Richardson, Scott, Edgeworth, and Austen in a thimble-sized survey of thc English novel.

Lady Blessington (CAT. 56)   *Mrs. B. Disraeli; formerly Mrs. Wyndham Lewis* (CAT. 52)

VII. LITERARY LIFE

ABOUT THE TIME she began to turn her attention to fiction, the "Author of Romance and Reality" (cat. 58) received one of the most important assignments of her career. Robert Fisher, known for publishing large-format books with finely executed engravings, was planning a new annual, composed of assorted prints accompanied by literary text as "illustration" for the pictures.

As a result of her work in *Forget Me Not* (cat. 25), *The Literary Souvenir* (cat. 27), *The Keepsake* (cat. 46), and other annuals, Landon had established a reputation for poetic illustration, and Fisher invited her to edit the new series. She could write the contents herself, or commission other authors to provide copy if she wished. Understandably, in light of her need for funds, she chose to write virtually all the illustrations herself. The first edition was scheduled for publication late in 1831, titled *Fisher's Drawing Room Scrap Book* for the year 1832, with 36 engravings, and accompanying text. The book was beautifully produced, a fine example of early Victorian book production, and it was an immediate success. Landon continued to edit these annuals through the volume for 1839, and had planned to complete the next (cat. 99) in West Africa.

Landon's eight volumes of the *Drawing Room Scrap Book* contain, amid a certain amount of merely routine work, a number of poems that have been greatly admired, such as the urban vignettes in "Scenes in London" (1836), or Landon's moving elegy on a contemporary poet, "Felicia Hemans" (1838). Unluckily, as with the *Book of Beauty*, reviewers considered the *Scrap Book* mainly to be a decorative *objet*, like a coffee-table book. Nevertheless, the poems were appreciated, especially in the United States, where publishers later brought out several collections from the volumes.

For Fisher, Landon also wrote: *The Easter Gift* (1832), with poems accompanying religious prints; and *A Birthday Tribute Addressed to Her Royal Highness the Princess Alexandrina Victoria on Attaining Her Eighteenth Year* (1837), published shortly before Victoria's accession. The volumes are beautifully produced, but the verse is un-inspired. Landon also wrote the contents for a large-format annual published by Ackermann, *Flowers of Loveliness* (1838) (cat. 89).

During these years Landon continued to contribute reviews to *The Literary Gazette* and to other periodicals, such as *The New Monthly Magazine*, and *The Court Journal* (begun in 1829). Since her articles are virtually all unsigned, the principal means of

OLD GORE HOUSE, IN 1830.

Gore House (CAT. 57)

L. E. L. (CAT. 55)

identifying her authorship is through allusions in letters or memoirs—or through the survival of her autograph manuscripts. Landon in her correspondence alludes to several of her articles and reviews, but most remain unidentified. One play that she is known to have attended and reviewed was J. B. Buckstone's *Uncle John* (cat. 49), a light but successful drama performed at the Haymarket Theatre (cat. 51) with William Farren (cat. 50), a popular comic actor, in the lead role.[28]

Landon also wrote anonymous profiles for magazines. A portion of Landon's manuscript survives to reveal her authorship of a profile of Benjamin Disraeli (cat. 53) for *The New Monthly Magazine* (1837).[29] She wrote a similar article on Bulwer (1831).[30] It seems likely that the profile of Lady Stepney in 1837 was also by Landon (they were close friends), and Landon may have written other profiles for the same magazine.

Another friend at this period was Mrs. Wyndham Lewis (cat. 52), known for lavish entertainments at her house, No. 1 Grosvenor Gate. Her first husband died in 1838 and a year later she married Disraeli. Landon was also close to Lady Blessington, *née* Marguerite Power (cat. 56), who, with Count D'Orsay, hosted receptions that made her home, Gore House (cat. 57), famous throughout the London literary world. If Mrs. Wyndam Lewis was known for her vivacity and charm, Lady Blessington was known for her warmth and kindness, which made guests feel as if she had singled out each one for special welcome. Another literary hostess and friend of Landon's was Mary Skinner, who lived at Croydon in a magnificent house, Shirley Park (cat. 54), where she entertained literary visitors.

VIII. SUMMER IN PARIS

IN JUNE of 1834 Landon was offered an opportunity to join friends on a trip to Paris. She had been planning a novel set amid the French Revolution, and could draw from Bentley some advance funds for *Francesca Carrara*, so on the spur of the moment she accepted. This seems to have been her only trip abroad until she left for Africa in 1838. From Paris she wrote a series of detailed letters to Jerdan, who later published them in his *Autobiography*. With these and letters to other friends, we have (for once) an extensive first-hand record of her day-to-day activities. She left England on June 19th by Channel steamer for Boulogne, and after a brief stopover, arrived in Paris a few days later.

Her reactions to Paris remind one of perennial comments by travelers about the lively scene on the boulevards, the stylish dress of the Parisians, the rush of traffic. Landon visited Galignani's bookshop (18 rue Vivienne), where one could buy English publications, and borrow books from a lending library. Galignani also published attractively printed editions of English works, priced far more cheaply than the regular editions, since British copyright law only protected works published in Britain, and had no authority over publications in other countries. Some of Landon's poems had been included in an anthology distributed by Galignani and others, *The Living Poets of England*, 2 vols. (1827). A similar collection, *The British Poets of the Nineteenth Century*, with an extensive section on Landon, was published at Frankfurt by H. L. Brœnner in 1828, and widely distributed on the Continent.

Landon visited standard tourist destinations, such as the Pantheon, Père Lachaise cemetery, the gardens of the Tuileries, and the galleries of the Louvre. While sightseeing she ran into Charles Arthur Gore, husband of the novelist Catherine Gore (cat. 61), an acquaintance of Landon's, and author of an illustrated guide, *Paris in 1841* (cat. 60), that gives a sharp impression of the city as it was near the time of Landon's visit.

One evening Landon attended a performance of the opera-ballet *La Tentation*, with music by Fromental Halévy (composer of *La Juive*, 1835), and saw the ballerina Pauline Duvernay dance "like an angel" (cat. 63). In a letter to William Jerdan, Landon recounts that afterward she and her friends "went and had ices at Tortoni's—such a brilliant scene" (cat. 64).[31] She was staying nearby at No. 30 rue Taitbout in a suite of rooms on a high floor looking out over neighboring gardens and *hôtels particuliers*, including that of James de Rothschild (19 rue Laffitte), and with a view of the picturesque windmills of Montmartre.

Landon's fame had preceded her, and even though—as she complained in one of her letters—there was "nobody"[32] in town during the summer, she had interesting meetings, as with the poet Heinrich Heine (cat. 66), who paid a call on her. This introduction had been arranged by Abraham Hayward (cat. 67, 68), a London acquaintance of Landon's, and translator of Goethe's *Faust*.

She also met Sainte-Beuve (cat. 70), Mérimée (cat. 71), and François Buloz. In 1832 Mme. Amable Tastu had published in the *Revue des Deux Mondes*, edited by Buloz,

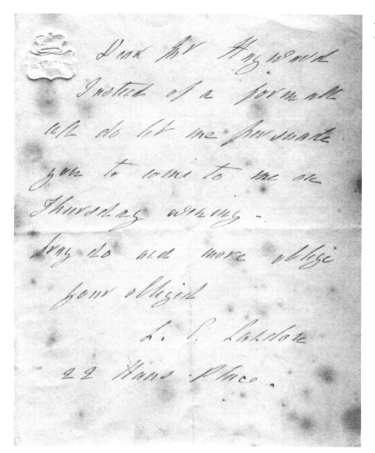

L. E. Landon, letter to Abraham Hayward (CAT. 68)

Seal of L. E. Landon (CAT. 68, *enlarged detail*)

Mme. Récamier (CAT. 72)

an article with French translations of Landon's poetry and a passage from *Romance and Reality* (cat. 62).[33] Odilon Barrot (cat. 69), a literary and political figure, became *cicerone* to Landon and her friends, for excursions to Notre Dame and the Jardin des Plantes (cat. 60). And she made the acquaintance of Antoine Fontaney (cat. 65), who seemed her ideal of what a young French poet should be—"pale, silent, *rêveur*, with a sort, too, of enthusiasm."[34]

Just before Landon was due to return to England she attended a reception at the *salon* of Juliette Récamier (cat. 72), "still beautiful, and with exquisite manners."[35] There Landon met the writer and French parliamentary leader Chateaubriand (cat. 73), and undoubtedly heard him read from his *Mémoires d'outre-tombe*. His readings were a regular feature of these afternoon gatherings, one of which is depicted in an etching by Auguste Hervieu for Frances Trollope's book on Paris (cat. 74). Over the mantelpiece hangs the dramatic painting by Gérard of Madame de Staël as Corinne improvising at the Cape of Misena. Landon had written English renderings of French improvisations for Isabel Hill's translation of *Corinne*, published in 1833 by Bentley (cat. 78) as No. XXIV of his Standard Novels, and many times reprinted in later years.

IX. TWO ENGAGEMENTS

SOMETIME AFTER Landon's return from Paris in 1834 she became engaged to John Forster (cat. 75), a young journalist who later gained prominence through his association with Landor and Dickens. On August 18th Landon saw Forster at the opera, where she heard the magnificent diva Giulia Grisi (cat. 77). Little is known precisely about the engagement except that around November 1835 it ended after Forster heard "rumours and stories"[36] about Landon and confronted her with them. In a letter to Bulwer (a friend of Forster's), she mentioned her fear of his "imperious and overbearing temper."[37]

The "stories" Forster heard included the old scandal from 1826 about Landon and

John Forster (CAT. 75)

Jerdan. William Maginn, and the artist Daniel Maclise (cat. 59) were now also rumored to have been involved with Landon. Maclise had drawn the lively portrait of Landon as "The Author of Romance and Reality," for *Fraser's Magazine*, 1833 (cat. 58). And he had recently drawn the somewhat romanticized frontispiece portrait (cat. 76) for Landon's *The Vow of the Peacock* (1835). The title poem provided a parallel poetic text for a large historical painting (on a medieval chivalric theme) that Maclise was exhibiting.

Landon's alleged involvement with Maginn led to events culminating in a duel on August 5, 1836 between Maginn and the Honourable Grantley Berkeley, M.P. Neither was wounded, but both made a splash in the London gossip.[38]

About this time, a certain distance seems to have affected Landon's relationship with Jerdan. Since the 1820s she had been working closely with him on *The Literary Gazette*, and he had been helping her negotiate with publishers, and editing work for her. In late 1834 and early 1835 she sent him for publication in the *Gazette* a series of translations from German poetry, including lyrics by Goethe, Schiller, Herder, and others, and a version of Goethe's *Egmont*.[39]

But after 1835 she published very little further signed work in the *Gazette*, and Jerdan's reviews become noticeably restrained. Surely it is not irrelevant that at this period he established an extramarital household with a young woman named Marion or Mary Ann (born about 1816 or 1817). They eventually had a sizeable family of children and she became known as Jerdan's wife, although his wife was still living.[40]

In the 1850s Nathaniel Hawthorne noted that Francis Bennoch (a friend and neighbor of Jerdan's), told him that Jerdan had "seduced" "innumerable women" and fathered "an infinity of illegitimate children." However, Bennoch stated that "Jerdan had assured him, on his honor, that L. E. L. had never yielded her virtue to him" and, Hawthorne notes, Bennoch added that he did not think Jerdan "would have denied it, had the case been otherwise."[41]

Among literary works of Landon's at this time are her novel *Francesca Carrara* (1834), mentioned earlier, and her collection of children's stories, with a few poems, *Traits and Trials of Early Life* (1836; 5th edition 1857) that includes "The History of a Child," based on Landon's early life at Trevor Park. Further autobiographical information by her appears in *The Book of Gems*, an anthology edited by her friend S. C. Hall, and issued late in 1837 as an annual for 1838.[42] She continued to edit *Fisher's Drawing Room Scrap Book* (cat. 99) and contributed to other annuals or gift books, including *Finden's Tableaux* (cat. 88), *Flowers of Loveliness* (cat. 89), and *Portraits of the Children of the Nobility* (cat. 90). She was also writing for Albert Schloss's *English Bijou Almanac*, a tiny miniature book about thumbnail size, with 64 pages of engraved text and pictures (cat. 87). Landon contributed five or six poems to each of the first four editions, published 1835–1838 (for 1836–1839).

REGINA'S MAIDS OF HONOUR.

Regina's Maids of Honour; L. E. L. is at left foreground (CAT. 79)

43 Connaught Street; formerly 28 Upper Berkeley Street West (CAT. 92; *photo by Margaret Baker*)

Landon figured among prominent women authors portrayed in *Fraser's Magazine* (January 1836) in a drawing titled "Regina's Maids of Honour" (cat. 79)—"Regina" was a nickname for the magazine—together with Anna Maria Hall, Lady Morgan, Caroline Norton, Lady Blessington, Jane Porter (author of *The Scottish Chiefs*), Harriet Martineau, and Mary Russell Mitford. In May 1837 *The New Monthly Magazine* published a profile of Landon with an engraved portrait by J. Wright (cat. 83).

The variety and number of Landon's literary assignments illustrates her position as a premier contributor to literary annuals; yet she needed the income to help family members such as her brother, for whom she was paying off a debt. He had graduated from Worcester College, Oxford (B.A. 1827; M.A. 1830), and had taken orders, but held only a low-paying curacy. In the spring of 1837 she also helped him campaign for election as secretary to the Literary Fund (later the Royal Literary Fund). Landon wrote to virtually everyone she knew who had a vote or might have influence. Her lobbying was successful, but in the end she felt that it had all been wasted effort since he was not able to hold a curacy at the same time, apparently because the secretaryship was a full-time administrative job.

In October 1836 Landon received a social invitation that would change her life. Through her friend Emma Roberts, Landon was invited to a party given by Mr. and Mrs. Matthew Forster (cat. 81) at their splendid residence, Belsize House, in Hampstead (cat. 80).[43] Matthew Forster was a leading merchant in the African trade, with ships sailing regularly between London and the Guinea Coast. One of the guests at the party would be George Maclean, president of the Council of Merchants, the governing body of the English region of the Gold Coast (now Ghana). His headquarters were at Cape Coast Castle, about 75 miles west of Accra.

Before the party, Landon read a memorandum about certain of Maclean's African exploits, and was impressed. For the occasion she wore a sash and hair-ribbon of the Maclean tartan. Brodie Cruickshank, author of a memoir of life on the Gold Coast, reports Landon's account of how she had initially imagined Maclean (cat. 82) as "some grey-haired officer," and when he entered the room she was surprised to see "what she was pleased to call 'a very fine and fashionable looking man in the prime of life.'"[44] Their acquaintance grew, and he eventually made a proposal of marriage. However, she suggested that they not consider themselves formally engaged for the moment, and that he think things over while he was in Scotland, where he would soon be going for an extended visit with his family.

In February 1837 Landon moved from 22 Hans Place to 28 Upper Berkeley Street West (the original house is still standing, now No. 43 Connaught Street, not far from Marble Arch) (cat. 92). She continued her literary work, finishing her novel *Ethel Churchill*, published in 1837, and editing or writing for several annuals.

Landon also attempted to fulfill a long-standing ambition to write a drama and have it staged. Her dramatic hero was a political leader in 14th-century Lucca, Castruccio Castrucani, who figures also in Mary Shelley's novel *Valperga*, and in Bulwer's *The Disowned*. Landon had wanted *Castruccio Castrucani; or, the Triumph of Lucca, a Tragedy*, submitted to the actor and theater manager William Macready (cat. 84) so that it could be considered for presentation at Covent Garden (cat. 85). But by the time her manuscript was ready, the schedule at the theater was fully booked.

Belsize House 1812 (CAT. 80; *courtesy Camden Local Studies and Archives Centre*)

L. E. L. (CAT. 83)

George Maclean (CAT. 82; *courtesy Veronica and John Maclean*)

Among that season's offerings was Bulwer's *The Lady of Lyons*, staged by Macready with Helen Faucit in the title role of Pauline (cat. 86), and himself as the male lead, Claude Melnotte. Landon attended a performance and called it "a succession of exquisite pictures."[45] And speaking of exquisite pictures, at about this time Maclise drew one of the best-known portraits of Landon, a minute version of which was published late in 1837 in Schloss's *Bijou Almanac for 1838* (cat. 87).

X. MARRIAGE AND AFRICA

LANDON'S engagement to George Maclean went through a crisis while he was in Scotland considering whether their marriage at this point was a wise course for him—or for her, given the unhealthful climate on the Guinea Coast. He had also heard rumors about Landon, but evidently dismissed them. At the same time, Landon had heard about Maclean's relationship with an African woman at Cape Coast. But he assured her that it was over, and had no legal standing. Eventually they settled their difficulties, and when he returned to London in 1838 they made plans for a June wedding. Because of her insistence that she wanted to return with him to Africa, they also began arrangements for her departure, and for her to continue her literary work while at Cape Coast, including long-distance writing for the *Drawing Room Scrap Book*.

Marriage and Africa

They were married on June 7, 1838 at St. Mary's Church, Bryanston Square (cat. 93), in a small private ceremony. Landon's brother officiated, and Bulwer gave away the bride; Bulwer, and Landon's cousin Mary Elizabeth Landon, from Aberford, signed the record as witnesses. Soon after the wedding, the couple left London, apparently to visit Maclean's family in Scotland, and perhaps also (if it could be accommodated in the itinerary) to visit Landon's relatives at Aberford, where two of her cousins had a double wedding scheduled for June 19th.[46] Landon's marriage was announced in London papers on June 23rd, and the couple arrived back in London on the 27th.

Landon's friends held a farewell party that evening, and the next day, from Crockford's Club (cat. 94), at 50 St. James's Street, she watched Queen Victoria's coronation procession (cat. 95). As soon as it passed by, Landon went to board the brig *Governor Maclean* (cat. 96), which was to take her and Maclean to Cape Coast. However, she found the accommodations totally unacceptable (perhaps the intended cabin was smelly, or the furnishings uncomfortable, or the position on the vessel was disadvantageous); new arrangements were ordered, and the couple made plans to board a few days later at Portsmouth, where they arrived on Monday, July 2nd, embarking the next afternoon.

The voyage seems to have gone relatively smoothly and uneventfully. They put in briefly at Madeira, and then continued past the Canary Islands, avoiding the dangerous sands of the Arguin Banks, site of the infamous wreck of the *Méduse* in 1816. They would also pass, at a distance, the Cape Verde Islands, and Cape Verde itself, before sailing by Sierra Leone and toward Cape Coast, which they reached on August 15th. They dropped anchor offshore (there was no harbor), and the next day, took small boats or canoes through the heavy surf to land on the beach.

Cape Coast Castle (cat. 97), today a well-known tourist attraction in Ghana, had changed hands many times over the centuries. It was originally built as a fort and holding place for cargo, including slaves, during the days of the slave trade (abolished by Britain in 1807). The curious name Cape Coast is from Portuguese *Cabo Corso*, originally *Cabo do Corso*, apparently after an early Portuguese navigator named Corso.[47]

As of 1838 the castle was inhabited mainly by a detachment of soldiers and a small administrative staff. The town to landward consisted of typical African dwellings interspersed with quaint colonial-style houses occupied by British and other merchants who traded in African products such as palm oil. Landon in letters home gives detailed descriptions of her surroundings and routines. The scene is also vividly sketched in *Eighteen Years on the Gold Coast* (1853), by Brodie Cruickshank, Maclean's right-hand man in Africa.

Brig Governor Maclean (CAT. 96; © *National Maritime Museum, Greenwich, London*)

Landon's and Maclean's rooms were seaward (left) of the hall at the top of the stairway in views of the castle. On the side of the hall opposite the stairway, a door opened onto an exterior gallery or walkway. Landon would get up at seven, have breakfast at eight, and after attending to household affairs, write until lunchtime, at one o'clock. In the afternoon she would continue writing. During this period at Cape Coast Castle, Landon worked on prose sketches of heroines from writings of Sir Walter Scott.

Dinner would be at seven in the evening, when Maclean would have returned from duties such as hearing cases as judicial officer. After they had dinner together he would play the violin, and she would read or do needlework, and at ten they would go to bed, although often Maclean would sit up late reading or writing.

Occasionally there were guests, or parties at merchants' houses, and on one occasion they went to the lagoon, where expatriates would go sailing in little boats or canoes that they had rigged up for their amusement. From Landon's letters one has the impression that once she and Maclean got settled in their quarters, she was interested in the surroundings, and happy in her situation.

In October, Cruickshank, who was stationed at the nearby British post at Anamaboe, paid a visit to Cape Coast Castle, where he planned to board the *Governor Maclean* and return to England on the 15th. The night before the brig was to sail, a dinner party was held at the castle. Cruickshank got ready to leave at eleven o'clock: "It was a fine clear night, and she strolled into the gallery, where we walked for half-an-hour."[48] Landon was, he recalled, "much struck with the beauty of the heavens in those latitudes at night, and said it was when looking at the moon and the stars that her thoughts oftenest reverted to home." But she added that he should not think she was "foolish" or "moonstruck," and that Matthew Forster had been quite mistaken in his opinion, before she left, that she would want to come right back to England.

The next morning brought shocking news. Her maid, Emily Bailey, found Landon unconscious in her room, collapsed on the floor against the door. It was soon determined that she was dead. There were no previous indications that Landon was suffering from a tropical disease or other serious illness. Maclean immediately called an inquest, and—after testimonies by Mrs. Bailey; by William Cobbold, the surgeon who had examined Landon; and by Maclean and others—the jury concluded that she had died from an accidental overdose of medicine that she had been taking, an open, empty bottle of which was found in the room near her body. The bottle was labeled hydrocyanic acid (or prussic acid), which at the time was often used in small doses for relief of internal "spasms," such as Landon had periodically suffered from (it is not clear what the present-day medical diagnosis would be).[49] Hydrocyanic acid can easily cause death if taken in more than the prescribed amount. She was buried late that afternoon in the courtyard of Cape Coast Castle, where her grave marked "L. E. L." (cat. 98) can be seen today, next to that of George Maclean (marked "G. M."), who died in 1847. In a niche in the wall facing the court is a marble memorial tablet to Landon.

News of Landon's death reached England in late December and appeared in an afternoon London newspaper, *The Courier,* on January 1, 1839 (the report was reprinted in *The Times* and other papers the following morning). Discussion immediately arose about whether Landon's death had really been accidental, or whether she might have committed suicide, or even been murdered by poisoning, perhaps through the African woman with whom Maclean earlier had had a liaison. Others suggested that Landon had died of a heart attack or some other sudden event connected with the "spasms" for which she was taking medication.

The discussion goes on still, and opinion seems to be as divided as ever. The less sensational explanation seems most reasonable: that the combination of her chronic "spasms," and the stresses of her new circumstances (marriage to Maclean, living in Africa), together with her habitual and possibly addictive use of strong medications and/or narcotics (including not only prussic acid, but also laudanum—opium in alcohol—which she is known to have used extensively) brought on a physical collapse that is difficult to attribute to one of these as the primary cause, but which seems most likely to have been accidental.[50]

At the time the news was announced, Landon's last regularly published poems appeared in the issue of *The New Monthly Magazine* for January 1839: "The Polar Star," and "Night at Sea" (both also in *The Courier* at this time). Soon memorial publications appeared, the most substantial of which was Laman Blanchard's *Life and Literary Remains of L. E. L.* (1841). Landon had appointed Blanchard as her literary executor.

Landon's poetry and fiction continued to be reprinted for decades after her death. Longman in 1839 and 1844 reprinted the four-volume edition of her *Poetical Works*, and in 1850 brought out a new edition (cat. 100), rearranged in two volumes, and reprinted in 1853, 1855, 1860, 1863 (dated 1864), and 1867.[51] Routledge then acquired the copyright, and in 1873 brought out a larger collection, with selections from *Fisher's Drawing Room Scrap Book,* and with the addition of poetic *Remains* as published by Blanchard in 1841. This edition was introduced and illustrated by the Pre-Raphaelite artist William Bell Scott (cat. 101), and reprinted in 1880 (in Routledge's Excelsior Series), and in 1884 (in Routledge's Red-Line Poets), and distributed in London, and in New York.[52] The edition remained available into the 1890s, and in 1990 was republished by Scholars' Facsimiles & Reprints, and continues in print today, as interest in Landon and her work, now revived, grows steadily.

———

THE GRAVE OF "L. E. L." IN CAPE COAST CASTLE

Grave of L. E. L. (CAT. 98)

CATALOGUE OF THE EXHIBITION

NOTE: Except as indicated in certain cases by credit lines, items shown in the exhibit, and listed in the following catalogue are from the author's collection. Individual prints that were originally published as part of a journal or book, are, where possible, catalogued with mention of the title of the larger work, even if the larger work is not in the collection; in such cases the catalogue entry usually reads: "Individual print, as published in: . . ." or similar wording (but in some cases the source has eluded research efforts). In cases where the complete journal or book containing the print is in the collection, the catalogue entry reads: "In: . . ." or similar wording. Details on works briefly cited in catalogue entries may be found at the end of the catalogue, under "Bibliography."

1. *Account of the Family of Landon of Monnington and Credenhill, Co. Hereford.* Compiled from notes and information collected by some members of the family. [N.p.]: Privately printed, 1912.

> The *Account* traces the family lines from Roger Landon, born circa 1555. His son John Landon, born circa 1574, is described as "Gentleman Yeoman of the Wine-cellar to James I. and Charles I." Letitia Landon's Cavalier sympathies are apparent in her novel *Francesca Carrara* (1834).

2. *James Landon. 1805.* Artist unidentified. Digital photograph by Paul Watt, 2010, of a framed reproduction (4¾ by 3¼″) hanging at the Church of St. Ricarius, Aberford, Yorkshire of a photo (original photo unavailable) of an original portrait (location unknown). Reproduced courtesy of the Rev. Bernard H. Fray, Priest-in-Charge of Aberford and Micklefield.

> James Landon (1764–1850), uncle of Letitia Elizabeth Landon, was a graduate of Worcester College, Oxford, 1787, and fellow of Oriel College. He was later named vicar of the Church of St. Ricarius, Aberford, Yorkshire.

3. *Doctor in Divinity* [in full dress]. T. Uwins, artist. I. Agar engraver. London: R. Ackermann, 1813. Aquatint, 13 x 10¾″. Individual print, as published in: *A History of the University of Oxford.* 2 vols. London: R. Ackermann, 1814. Vol. 2, plate 1, between pp. 258 and 259.

> Whittington Landon, D.D. (bpt. 1758; d. 1839), uncle of Letitia Elizabeth Landon, was a graduate of Worcester College, Oxford, 1779; later named provost of Worcester College, and dean of Exeter. Ackermann gives no personal identifications for these illustrations, but a contemporary wrote them in a copy of the book in 1814. See article by John Pickford in *Notes and Queries* (July 6, 1878).

4. *Birthplace of Miss Landon.* Wood engraving in text, 3¼ x 2½″. In: *Cyclopædia of English Literature.* Edited by Robert Chambers. 2 vols. Edinburgh: William and Robert Chambers, 1844. Vol. 2, p. 449.

> No. 25 Hans Place, Chelsea, where Landon was born on August 14, 1802, was designed by Henry Holland, and built in the 1770s as part of the development of the area then known as Hans Town (for Sir Hans Sloane).

5. *Chelsea Old Church, and Sir Han [sic] Sloane's Monument.* Tho. H. Shepherd, artist. R. Acon, engraver [n.p., n.d.]. Steel engraving, 5½ x 8½″. Individual print, as published in: Thomas H. Shepherd, *London and Its Environs in the Nineteenth Century.* Series the first. London: Jones & Co., 1829.

> The Church of St. Luke (or St. Luke and All Saints), known as Chelsea Old Church, London, where Landon was baptized on October 18, 1805. Her mother and father were married there June 15, 1797.

6. *Map 4. Containing the Old Inclosures from Greenhill Grove & Liens Down to East Barnet Church.* Tho. Tatham Commissioner. Thomas Denton, Surveyor. Digital photograph provided by and reproduced with permission of Hertfordshire Archives & Local Studies. Manuscript enclosure map drawn in 1818 to scale of 1 inch to 6 chains (1 chain = 66 feet, or ¹/₈₀ mile); dimensions of original map, 26 x 20″.

> This enlarged detail shows the footprint of the house where Landon lived as a child, Trevor Park, demolished around 1819; no view is known. The L-shaped house is near Church Hill Road; to the south is the Church of St. Mary the Virgin (interior of nave, 40 x 19 ft.; walls 3 ft. thick). By estimate, the house would have measured about 43 ft. on the side facing the church, and about 36 ft. on the side facing the road. (Compare Water End House, cat. 9.)

7. *East Barnet Church, Herts.* Drawn & Engraved by I. Hassell. London: Hassell, 1817. Engraving, colored, as issued, 5⅛ x 8¼″. Individual print, as published in: J. Hassell, *Picturesque Rides and Walks, with Excursions by Water, Thirty Miles Round the British Metropolis.* 2 vols. London: J. Hassell, 1817–1818. Vol. 1 (1817), facing p. 193.

> The Church of St. Mary the Virgin, East Barnet, was adjacent to Trevor Park, where Landon lived from about 1809 to about 1816. See cat. 6. She mentions this church in her autobiographical story "The History of a Child."

8. Church of St. Mary the Virgin, near Landon's Childhood Home, circa 1807. [Samuel Woodburn, artist.] [James] Newton, engraver [n.p., n.d]. Copper engraving, 6¾ x 9⅛″; plate size, 6 x 7⅞″; image size, 4⅞ x 7″.

> According to the local historian F. C. Cass, "a wooden turret surmounting the west end in 1794, and conspicuous in Woodburn's illustration, was replaced between that date and 1817

by a sort of octagon belfry" (p. 171); compare cat. 7. When Landon's friend Emma Roberts visited friends near East Barnet, she recounts, Landon asked her to make "a pilgrimage to the spot which once was Trevor Park, and not fail to think of her as I stood among the gravestones of the village churchyard" (p. 9). This view (apparently a proof before letters) is very similar to that published in: Samuel Woodburn, *Ecclesiastical Topography: A Collection of One Hundred Views of Churches in the Environs of London*, 2 vols. (London: Cadell & Davies et al., and S. Woodburn, 1807), plate no. 38, signed in lower right corner "Newton sculpt." and with title "East Barnet, Herts.," and credit, "London: S. Woodburn, 1807."

9. *Water End House.* "RS" [Richard Smythson], artist. W. Measom, engraver. Wood engraving in text, 4½ x 6″. In: John Edward Cussans, *History of Hertfordshire.* 3 vols. London: Chatto and Windus, 1870–1881. Vol. 3, [part 2] Hundred of Cashio (1881), p. 222.

> Water End House, Wheathampstead (formerly Sandridge), Hertfordshire, stands about 12 miles north of East Barnet. Of this "fine old brick mansion," built around 1610, Cussans notes "a good oak staircase, a little pannelling, and the usual long garret extending the whole length of the building." Landon's home in East Barnet, Trevor Park, new in 1611, was "gabled," and from its L-shaped footprint (cat. 6), and from details in Landon's autobiographical story "The History of a Child," it is plausible that Trevor Park (of which no illustration is known) may have resembled Water End House, also gabled, L-shaped, and built nearby to similar dimensions during this period.

10. Walter Scott. *The Lay of the Last Minstrel, a Poem.* 13th edition. London: Longman, Hurst, Rees, Orme, and Brown, 1812. First published 1805.

> As a child at Trevor Park, Landon especially loved Scott's poetry. This volume, in period binding, is stamped in gilt with a monogram "LEL" on front and back covers. Whether it ever belonged to the poet L. E. L. is impossible to say, for it has no inscriptions except a long-ago British bookseller's penciled price, "6/–" and underneath it, also in pencil, "LEL" (which could suggest the bookseller's awareness of an association with Landon).

11. [George Walker.] *Travels of Sylvester Tramper through the Interior of the South of Africa: With the Adventures & Accidents That He Encountered in a Journey of More Than Two Thousand Miles through Those Unknown Wildernesses, Constantly Exposed to Danger from Beasts of Prey, and the Attacks of Savages.* Second Edition. London: G. Walker, 1813.

> When Landon was living at Trevor Park, East Barnet, her father gave her a copy of *Sylvester Tramper,* about adventures in southern Africa, where he had voyaged in earlier years.

12. Richard Savage. *The Poetical Works of Richard Savage.* With the life of the author, by Doctor Johnson. Cooke's Edition. London: Printed by J. Wright for C. Cooke [n.d., but c. 1802].

At Trevor Park, Landon read volumes of Cooke's editions of poets and novelists. This copy is in paper-covered boards as issued, with an advertisement leaf listing the titles and prices of volumes in the series.

13. *Miss Landon's Residence at Old Brompton.* Wood engraving in text, 3¾ x 4½″. In: S. C. Hall, *A Book of Memories of Great Men and Women of the Age, from Personal Acquaintance.* London: Virtue & Co., 1871. Page 266.

> Brompton Villa, where Landon lived from about 1817 to 1820, was built circa 1770. An advertisement in the *Morning Chronicle* (August 5, 1820), p. 4, describes it as "a modern brick-built House, containing nine bed chambers, two dressing rooms, a handsome drawing room, breakfast and dining room, good kitchen, larders, store room, wash-house, and cellaring; double coach-house, six-stall stable, cow-house, and piggeries, pleasure grounds, productive kitchen garden, and close of rich Meadow Land...." The Landons regarded this, after Trevor Park, as a severe retrenchment in life-style.

14. *The Editor of the Literary Gazette.* Daniel Maclise, artist. London: J. Fraser [1830]. Reproduction of lithograph, 10½ x 8″. Individual print, issued independently, n.d. The original lithograph, on different paper (8½ x 5″), appeared in *Fraser's Magazine,* vol. 1, no. 5 (June 1830), facing p. 605.

> Jerdan was No. I in *Fraser's* "Gallery of Illustrious Literary Characters" from drawings by "Alfred Croquis," i.e., Daniel Maclise. The headnote (by William Maginn) begins: "On the opposite page sits William Jerdan, the Editor of the *Literary Gazette,* reduced from six feet high to as many inches—but still the very man. We defy pencil or graver to produce a more wonderful likeness...." Jerdan is described as reading a proof of the *Gazette,* "with scrutinising eye, in quest of *literals.*"

15. Letitia Elizabeth Landon. Autograph letter signed, undated, to William Jerdan.

> Dear Sir
> In the utter desperation of dust and disorder, I have procured a messenger—and beg to return you a thousand and one books. Those tied with a blue string are to be dispatched to Hookham's those tied with white, are what came last week, and the rest rubbish—pray call soon after three for I am going to Harrow this evening—and want to talk to you
> Yours trul
> L E L
>
> The letter (addressed "W Jerdan Esq") closes thus, obviously in haste. The books must have been review copies of works that Landon had reviewed for *The Literary Gazette.* Hookham's was a circulating library in London. A possible date might be suggested by Landon's visit in 1832 to Frances Trollope, who lived in Harrow.

16. *The London Literary Gazette,* no. 552 (Saturday, August 18, 1827), pp. 529–544. Individual issue of the journal.

> Landon's first published poems appeared in 1820 in *The Literary Gazette,* edited by William Jerdan. For most of her career she contributed original poems, as well as anonymous articles and reviews. This number has two poems by "L. E. L." ("Broken Vows" and "Euthenasia"), and one by Jerdan ("The Seasons of One Year"), signed "Teutha" (Celtic name for the River Tweed, and a *nom de plume* of Jerdan's, alluding to his birthplace, Kelso, Scotland). This journal was published under two similar names: *The London Literary Gazette* and *The Literary Gazette.* Copies printed on plain (unstamped) paper, were sold by retailers at 8*d.* per copy, and titled *The London Literary Gazette.* Copies printed on paper with a pre-printed red stamp in the corner of the sheet (reading "FOUR PENCE" indicating pre-payment of duty on newspapers) were sent by post, priced at one shilling and titled *The Literary Gazette.* The journal is referred to as *The Literary Gazette,* since the literary contents were the same for both.

17. Letitia Elizabeth Landon. *The Fate of Adelaide, a Swiss Romantic Tale; and Other Poems.* London: John Warren, 1821. Facsimile, edited by F. J. Sypher. Ann Arbor, Michigan: Scholars' Facsimiles & Reprints, 1990.

> *The Fate of Adelaide,* Landon's first published book, was not included in collected editions of her work, and was not reprinted until 1990, when Scholars' Facsimiles & Reprints brought out this volume.

18. *Mrs. Siddons.* George Romney, artist. Halftone, 8½ x 5½". In: Mrs. Clement Parsons, *The Incomparable Siddons.* London: Methuen & Co., 1909. Facing p. 38.

> Landon dedicated her first book, *The Fate of Adelaide* (1821), "To Mrs. Siddons," whose "sanction" was "the greatest encouragement. . . ." Signed "L. E. L." Sarah Siddons, born in 1775, was an icon of the British dramatic stage, revered for her powerful performances in roles such as Lady Macbeth.

19. John Howard Payne. *Charles the Second; or, the Merry Monarch. A Comedy, in Three Acts, (with some songs): First Performed at the Theatre Royal, Covent Garden, on Thursday Evening, May 27, 1824.* London: Longman, Hurst, Rees, Orme, Brown, and Green, 1824.

> In the preface to *Charles the Second,* dated June 5, 1824, Payne concludes: ". . . the Songs were supplied, during my absence, by, as I am informed, 'a very amiable and accomplished young lady,' whose concealment of her name shows that her modesty is equal to her merit." The "young lady" was L. E. L., whose initials appear on the sheet music (cat. 20). Landon supplied three songs: "Oh! not when other eyes may read"; "Love one day" (duet); and "Not in the pictured halls." She mentions and quotes from the play in her novel *Romance and Reality* (vol. 2, ch. 19, p. 273). The authorship of the songs is identified only in the separately-published sheet music.

20. Henry R. Bishop. *Love, one day. Duetto. Sung by Miss M. Tree & Mr. Duruset, The Poetry by L. E. L., in the Comedy of Charles the Second, at the Theatre Royal Covent Garden.* Dublin: Goulding D'Almaine & Co. [n.d.; paper watermarked 1827].

> Maria Tree in 1823 had won over the theatrical world in the title role of *Clari; or, the Maid of Milan* with Bishop's song "Home, Sweet Home." Landon's songs for *Charles the Second* were not credited to her in the play, and she never brought this material together to be reprinted. Her authorship came to my attention in the course of identifying and cataloguing nearly 100 musical compositions based on words by Landon.

21. Letitia Elizabeth Landon. *The Improvisatrice; and Other Poems.* By L. E. L. With embellishments. London: Hurst, Robinson and Co.; Edinburgh: Archibald Constable and Co., 1824. Second edition.

> Landon's *The Improvisatrice* was published July 18, 1824. A second edition appeared in September, and a third before the end of the year; three more followed in the next year, and a seventh edition in 1826. The principal difference between the first and second editions is that the first has seven plates, while the second has two.

22. *Archibald Constable.* Wood engraving in text, 3¼ x 3¼". In: "Archibald Constable and His Friends," *Harper's New Monthly Magazine,* no. 286 (March 1874), p. 501. An original unbound number of the magazine as issued.

> Archibald Constable was one of Landon's publishers for *The Improvisatrice* (cat. 21). In the fall of 1825 Landon traveled to visit her uncle James Landon in Yorkshire, with Constable in his private carriage. With them was Richard Milliken, a young man who noted her conversation in his diary.

23. Letitia Elizabeth Landon. Autograph manuscript, signed "L. E. L." Headed "Lines on the Princess Charlotte's Mausoleum" [1823].

> The Princess Charlotte, daughter of King George IV, died in 1817, at the age of 21. At Claremont she had begun construction of a decorative Gothic temple, later completed as a memorial to her. Landon's poem on the Princess Charlotte's Mausoleum was printed in Ackermann's new annual, *Forget Me Not* for 1824.

24. *Princess Charlotte of Wales. Ob. 1817.* A. E. Chalon, artist. H. T. Ryall, engraver. London: Harding and Lepard, 1833. Steel engraving, 10¾ x 6⅞". Individual print, as published in: Edmund Lodge, *Portraits of Illustrious Personages of Great Britain.* London: Harding and Lepard, 1835. Vol. 12, portrait no. 234.

> The Princess Charlotte was born in 1796, the only child of George IV and Queen Caroline, and married Leopold of Saxe-Coburg-Saalfeld in 1816. The following year, she and an infant son died in childbirth. Her child would have been heir to the throne.

Catalogue

25. *Forget Me Not; a Christmas and New Year's Present, for 1824.* London: R. Ackermann [published late 1823].

> *Forget Me Not* was the first of the English literary annuals of the period. This, the second annual issue, includes Landon's poem (cat. 23) retitled "Lines on the Mausoleum of the Princess Charlotte at Claremont," and two engraved plates of the monument. Also included is Landon's poem "Ellen; a Fragment."

26. *Alaric A Watts.* Henry Howard, artist. Anna Lea Merritt, etcher. Etching, 7⅜ x 5″. In: Alaric Alfred Watts, *Alaric Watts: A Narrative of His Life.* 2 vols. London: Richard Bentley and Son, 1884. Frontispiece to volume 1.

> Landon corresponded with Watts about her forthcoming poem *The Troubadour,* and about the new annual that Watts was editing, *The Literary Souvenir,* which made its debut in late 1824 with the volume for 1825. Landon became a regular contributor to the series. Anna Lea Merritt (1844–1930), who made this etching, was born in the United States but pursued her career in England from 1872, and became known for her etchings, especially portraits.

27. *The Literary Souvenir; or, Cabinet of Poetry and Romance.* Edited by Alaric A. Watts. London: Longman, Rees, Orme, Brown, & Green, 1828 [published late 1827].

> This issue of *The Literary Souvenir* contains Landon's "Juliet after the Masquerade," composed to accompany an engraving by Charles Rolls of a picture by Henry Thomson on the same theme. The poem is a reworking of one in *The Troubadour* (1825). Also by Landon in this annual are: "The Lost Star," "Ballad," "The Adieu," and "Love Tormenting the Soul."

28. Letitia Elizabeth Landon. *The Troubadour; Catalogue of Pictures, and Historical Sketches.* London: Hurst, Robinson and Co.; Edinburgh: A. Constable and Co., 1825. In original gray paper boards, with printed paper label on spine, reading: "[rule] | THE | TROUBADOUR, | AND | OTHER POEMS. | [rule] | *Price,* 10*s.* 6*d.* | [rule]."

> *The Troubadour,* Landon's second big success, had a printed dedication: "To William Jerdan, Esq. this work, so much indebted to his kind surveillance, is inscribed, by the obliged author, L. E. L." On the verso of the half-title of this copy is inscribed, in the handwriting of William Jerdan, a 12-line poem titled "To L. E. L." (first line: "Lady! should friends forsake, and hearts once kind"). On p. 308 is a ms. annotation in Jerdan's hand; penciled underneath it is: "Mss. By William Jerdan." The front free endpaper and the frontispiece plate are lacking. One wonders if perhaps this copy was originally inscribed by L. E. L. to Jerdan (who then copied his poem into it), and those leaves were removed by an autograph collector. The uncut pages measure 4¼ x 6⅞″.

29. *L. E. L. Æt. 26.* H. W. Pickersgill, artist. H. Robinson, engraver. Steel engraving, 7 x 4⅜″. In: *The Autobiography of William Jerdan.* 4 vols. London: Arthur Hall, Virtue & Co., 1852–1853. Vol. 3 (1853), frontispiece.

Of this portrait of Landon, S. C. Hall, in an article on portraits of Landon, says: "We always considered it a good likeness, though not an agreeable one; and it was never in favour with her friends" (pp. 3–4). Pickersgill later executed another portrait of Landon (cat. 55).

30. *Miss Benger. Author of the "Memoir of Mary Queen of Scots, &c."* Wegeman, artist. Woolnoth, engraver [n.p., n.d.]. Steel engraving, 6¼ x 4⅝″. Individual print, as published in: *The Ladies' Monthly Museum*, vol. 21, no. 3 (March 1825), facing p. 121.

> Early in her literary career, Landon joined the literary circle of Elizabeth Benger, an author and hostess, and Elizabeth Isabella Spence.

31. *Anna Maria Hall.* J. Hayter, artist. C. E. Wagstaff, engraver. London: Henry Colburn, 1838. Steel engraving, 8⅞ x 5½″. In: *The New Monthly Magazine*, vol. 53, no. 212 (August 1838), frontispiece.

> In Anna Maria Hall's novel *A Woman's Story*, 3 vols. (London: Hurst & Blackett, 1857), the central character is modeled on Landon. The narrator speaks of "the earnestness" of her "devotion to Helen Lyndsey; her name was like a stroke of electricity, throbbing and exciting, savouring more of pain than pleasure." "Had I been a man, the world would have said I was in love with Helen." (Vol. 2, ch. 3, pp. 38, 40.) Landon seems to have had a similar impact upon many women and men.

32. *S. C. Hall.* Paul de la Roche, artist. Lumb Stocks, engraver. Steel engraving, 8½ x 5½″. In: S. C. Hall, *Retrospect of a Long Life: from 1815 to 1883.* 2 vols. London: Richard Bentley & Son, 1883. Vol. 1, frontispiece.

> S. C. Hall edited periodicals and annuals, and his wife Anna Maria Hall wrote novels and stories, primarily of Irish life. At their home on Sloane Street, Landon was a frequent guest, as were many active writers and artists of the day.

33. *"The Doctor."* Daniel Maclise, artist. London: James Fraser [1830]. Lithograph, 8½ x 5″. In: *Fraser's Magazine*, vol. 2, no. 12 (January 1831), facing p. 716.

> William Maginn, a brilliant journalist for *Fraser's Magazine*, was on friendly terms with Landon from about 1823. In 1835 their names were romantically linked in a rumor that proved damaging for both.

34. *Rosina Lytton.* A. E. Chalon, artist (1852). I. Jewell Penstone, engraver. London: Swan Sonnenschein & Co., 1887. Gravure, 8¾ x 5⅜″. In: Louisa Devey, *Life of Rosina, Lady Lytton.* London: Swan Sonnenschein, Lowrey & Co., 1887.

> Rosina Wheeler (later Lady Lytton), an early, passionately-attached friend of Landon's, married Edward Bulwer in 1827 in an impetuous love match. The marriage broke up around 1833 and she afterward accused Landon of "intriguing with my infamous husband" (p. 127).

35. [Bulwer] *The Author of "Pelham."* F. Say, artist. Boston: Kane & Co's Atheneum, 1831. Lithograph, 11¾ x 9½". Individual print, as published in: *The Atheneum, or Spirit of the English Magazines,* series 4, vol. 1, no. 8 (August 1, 1831), facing p. 426.

> Bulwer and Landon were close and loyal friends. In general, little credence has been given to the accusation by Rosina Bulwer (Lady Lytton) that they were more than friends.

36. *L. E. L.* Adam Buck, artist. I. Hawksworth, engraver. London: Sherwood Gilbert & Piper, 1826. Steel engraving, 6 x 3⅞". In: *Poetry and Poets.* Edited and compiled by Richard Ryan. 3 vols. London: Sherwood, Gilbert, & Piper, 1826. Vol. 2, frontispiece.

> Adam Buck's portrait of Landon, as shown in this engraving, looks nothing like other portraits of her. The reviewer for *The Literary Gazette,* no. 532 (March 31, 1827) commented in a notice of Ryan's anthology (with a brief section on Landon) that the portrait of her "is a sheer invention, and must belong, if to any one, to some other lady."

37. *No. 22 Hans Place.* [F. W. Fairholt, artist.] Wood engraving in text, 2 x 1¾". In: T. Crofton Croker, "A Walk from London to Fulham," *Fraser's Magazine,* vol. 31, no. 181 (January 1845), p. 5.

> Landon moved to 22 Hans Place in late December 1826, and lived there until early 1837. There the Lance sisters ran a day school, and rented rooms to women boarders. The one-story extension was used as the schoolroom, and in off-hours Landon received visitors there, and even held dance parties. *A Walk from London to Fulham* first appeared as a series of magazine articles, was published in book form in 1860, and reprinted in 1896. This is a custom-bound volume comprising the original magazine articles published in 1845 in *Fraser's Magazine.*

38. *Attic, No. 22 Hans Place.* [F. W. Fairholt, artist.] Wood engraving in text, 1¾ x 1½". In: T. Crofton Croker, "A Walk from London to Fulham," *Fraser's Magazine,* vol. 31, no. 181 (January 1845), p. 6. From same volume as above (cat. 37).

> Landon in her novel *Ethel Churchill* (1837) wrote: "A history of the *how* and *where* works of imagination have been produced would often be more extraordinary than the works themselves." (Vol. 1, ch. 16, p. 163.) Readers imagined Landon in a luxurious chamber, hung with silks; the reality was this garret, where she wrote at a lap-desk on a little dressing table. The window overlooked Hans Place.

39. Letitia Elizabeth Landon. *The Golden Violet, with Its Tales of Romance and Chivalry: and Other Poems.* London: Longman, Rees, Orme, Brown, and Green, 1827 [published late 1826].

> Landon's *The Golden Violet* continues the themes of *The Troubadour,* but did not go into a second edition at this time. She dedicated the book to her uncle the Reverend James

Landon, in Yorkshire, where she worked on it during the summer of 1826. Contemporary paper-covered boards (spine rebacked; printed paper label not original); the uncut pages measure 4⅜ x 6¾".

40. Letitia Elizabeth Landon. *The Venetian Bracelet, The Lost Pleiad, A History of the Lyre, and Other Poems.* London: Longman, Rees, Orme, Brown, and Green, 1829.

Landon's *The Venetian Bracelet* contains poems that present her autobiography in symbolic terms. Because the volume sold poorly, the publisher had copies on hand for years. Landon soon turned to fiction. The pages on this copy are uncut, 4¼ x 6¾".

41. *The Old Vicarage.* Digital photograph by Paul Watt, 2010, of a framed reproduction (6 by 7½") hanging at the Church of St. Ricarius, Aberford, Yorkshire, from an original photographic print (unavailable). Reproduced courtesy of the Rev. Bernard H. Fray, Priest-in-Charge of Aberford and Micklefield.

Of the residence of Landon's uncle James Landon, the vicarage at Aberford, Yorkshire, Landon remarked in one of her letters (mentioned in Part I) that the stairs and hallways of the house were so bewildering that she needed a chart. Her traveling companion in 1825, Richard Milliken, noted that to reach the house one had to go through a churchyard. The original photo was taken in or before 1861, when the house was demolished.

42. *The Old Parish Church.* Digital photograph by Paul Watt, 2010, of a framed reproduction (6 by 7½") hanging at the Church of St. Ricarius, Aberford, Yorkshire, from an original photographic print (unavailable). Reproduced courtesy of the Rev. Bernard H. Fray, Priest-in-Charge of Aberford and Micklefield.

At the Church of St. Ricarius, Aberford, Yorkshire are the graves of Landon's uncle and aunt, James Landon and Anne Bainbridge Landon, as well as a memorial window to Anne Bainbridge Landon (d. 1861). The original photo was taken in or before 1861, when the church was extensively rebuilt.

43. *Kilchurn Castle.* Copley Fielding, artist. I. Jeavons, engraver. London: Chapman & Hall, 1833. Steel engraving, 6⅜ x 9¼". Individual print as published in: *Portraits of the Principal Female Characters in the Waverley Novels.* London: Chapman & Hall, 1833.

Landon's poem "Follow Me"—inspired by her visit to Kilchurn Castle, an abandoned structure on an island in Loch Awe, in Scotland—appeared in *The Literary Gazette*, no. 709 (August 21, 1830), and was reprinted in Landon's volume *The Vow of the Peacock* (1835) (cat. 76). The title is the motto of a branch of the Campbell family; Landon was struck by the irony in the words "Follow Me" carved in the lintel over the entrance to the ruin.

44. Letitia Elizabeth Landon. *Romance and Reality*. By L. E. L. Author of "The Improvisatrice," "The Venetian Bracelet," &c. &c. 3 vols. London: Henry Colburn and Richard Bentley, 1831.

> *Romance and Reality*, Landon's first novel, later went through many editions in Britain and the United States, to 1871. Portions, translated into French and German, appeared in Paris and Leipzig periodicals, and the full text appeared in Dutch as *Waarheid en verdichting* (1848). *Romance and Reality* has not been the first choice of critics, but it has clearly been popular among her readers.

45. *The New Athenæum, Waterloo Place*. Tho. H. Shepherd, artist. J. Tingle, engraver. Steel engraving, 5¼ x 8¼″. Individual print, as published in: Thomas H. Shepherd, *London and Its Environs in the Nineteenth Century*. Series the first. London: Jones & Co., 1829.

> In volume 1, chapter 22 of *Romance and Reality*, Emily, the heroine, attends a reception at the Athenæum, where she meets literary figures modeled on contemporaries such as Bulwer and his wife Rosina. Landon herself may well have attended a similar event at the Athenæum.

46. *The Keepsake*, for 1838. New Series. London: Longman, Orme, Brown, Green and Longmans [published late 1837].

> In this volume of *The Keepsake* all the contributions appeared anonymously. The opening piece, the short story "The Royal Marriage; or, Political Expedience," is attributed to Landon because of the survival of her autograph manuscript.

47. *Heath's Book of Beauty*. M.DCCC.XXXIII. By L. E. L. London: Longman, Rees, Orme, Brown, Green, and Longman [published late 1832].

> Landon wrote the entire contents for *Heath's Book of Beauty* for 1833 (first in the series), mostly short stories of excellent quality. Lady Blessington edited the volumes for 1834 through 1849.

48. William Sterndale Bennett. "Two Songs." [London:] Greening's Music Ltd. [c. 1900; first published 1841]. Cover art by Charles Folkard. The first song is "Wind, Wave and Bark," with (uncredited) words from Landon's "Love's Motto";

> *and:*

Eliza Flower. "L.E.L.'s Song 'Sleep, heart of mine!'" London: J. Alfred Novello [c. 1839]. Words from Landon's "The Ancestress";

> *and:*

George Linley. "Constance." London: Chappell & Co. [c. 1861; first published c. 1837]. Cover art by J. Brandard. Words (uncredited) from a poem in Landon's novel *Ethel*

Churchill (1837), vol. 1, ch. 12; a prose passage from the novel (uncredited; from vol. 1, ch. 13, pp. 128–129) is quoted at the head of the song (Constance is a character in the novel);

and:

Alexander Roche. "How many loved and honored thee." Words by L. E. Landon. London: J. Dean [1835]. From Landon's "Stanzas on the Death of Mrs. Hemans."

> Linley's song "Constance" was often reprinted, as was Sterndale Bennett's "Wind, Wave and Bark." Nearly 100 musical compositions based on words by Landon have been identified, and there are undoubtedly many more.

49. J. B. Buckstone. *Uncle John. A Petite Comedy, in Two Acts.* London: John Miller, 1833.

> Landon attended Buckstone's play and reviewed it for *The Literary Gazette*, no. 874 (October 19, 1833), as a "lively and successful farce." The article, like nearly all her reviews, is unsigned, but her authorship is attested by her comments about the play in a letter of October 1833 to Mrs. Wyndham Lewis.

50. *Mr. William Farren of the Theatre Royal Covent Garden.* George Clint, artist. J. Thomson, engraver. London: European Magazine, 1822. Steel engraving, 7 x 4¼″. Individual print, as published in *The European Magazine, and London Review*, vol. 81, no. 2 (February 1822), facing p. 99.

> Of Farren's performance as Uncle John, Landon writes in her review for *The Literary Gazette*, no. 874 (October 19, 1833): "Farren, whose face is a complete Portrait Annual, has the principal character; and one of the most original and entertaining which even he ever made seem like a familiar acquaintance, with this single exception, that few of one's familiar acquaintance are very amusing; while he always is."

51. *United Service Military Club House, Haymarket Theatre, & Part of the Opera Colonade, from Regent Street.* Thos. H. Shepherd, artist. Wm. Wallis, engraver. London: Jones & Co., 1827. Steel engraving, 5⅛ x 7¾″. Individual print, as published in: Thomas H. Shepherd, *Metropolitan Improvements*. London: Jones & Co., 1827.

> At the Haymarket Theatre, Landon attended an early performance of *Uncle John*, which she reviewed for *The Literary Gazette*.

52. *Mrs. B. D'Israeli.* A. E. Chalon, artist. W. H. Mote, engraver. London: Longman & Co., 1840. Steel engraving, 8¾ x 6⅛″. Individual print, as published in: *Heath's Book of Beauty* for 1841, edited by the Countess of Blessington. London: Longman, Orme, Brown, Green & Longman [published late 1840].

Landon and Mrs. Wyndham Lewis (later Mrs. Disraeli) especially enjoyed going to the theater together. Landon dedicated her novel *Francesca Carrara* "To Mrs. Wyndham Lewis"—"a slight remembrance of your kindness to Your affectionate L. E. L."

53. *Benj Disraeli.* D'Orsay, artist. London: Henry Colburn, 1837. Steel engraving, 8¾ x 5½". In: *The New Monthly Magazine*, vol. 49, no. 196 (April 1837), facing p. 458, as an illustration with "Memoir of B. D'Israeli, Esq." by a Correspondent [L. E. Landon].

> Landon and Disraeli both attended parties given by Mr. and Mrs. Wyndham Lewis. Wyndham Lewis died in 1838, and a year later his widow and Disraeli were married. Count D'Orsay drew many portraits of contemporaries, but was best known as a pattern of elegance, and exemplar of the Regency dandy. With Lady Blessington he presided over their salon at Gore House.

54. *Shirley House, Seat of J. Maberly, Esq*. M.P.* J. Fletcher, artist. Castles, engraver. London: I. T. Hinton [1831]. Steel engraving, 5¼ x 8". Individual print, as published in *The Picturesque Beauties of the Counties of Surrey and Sussex*. London: I. T. Hinton, 1831.

> Landon's friend Mary Skinner gave literary parties at Shirley Park, her house at Croydon, where she lived from circa 1833, when her husband Samuel Skinner purchased the property from the assigns of John Maberley (the usual spelling). Guests included Thomas Moore, Joanna Baillie, Jane Porter, Julia Pardoe, and the American journalist Nathaniel Parker Willis.

55. *L. E. L.* H. W. Pickersgill, artist. C. Cook, engraver. London: Richard Bentley, 1848. Steel engraving, 8⅞ x 5½". In: *Bentley's Miscellany*, vol. 23 (January to June 1848), facing p. 534, with unsigned biographical sketch, pp. 532–534.

> *Bentley's Miscellany* was also the place of publication of a memoir of Landon by her friend Katherine Byerley Thomson, "Memorials of the Departed Great; by a Middle-Aged Man," vol. 17 (1845), pp. 182–191. She revised it for publication in her *Recollections of Literary Characters and Celebrated Places*, 2 vols. (London: Richard Bentley, 1854), and further revised it for *The Queens of Society*, 2 vols. (London: James Hogg, 1860).

56. *Marguerite, Countess of Blessington.* A. E. Chalon, artist. J. J. Hinchliff, engraver [n.p., n.d.]. Steel engraving, 10⅞ x 8⅛". Individual print, as published in: R. R. Madden, *The Literary Life and Correspondence of the Countess of Blessington*. 2nd edition. 3 vols. London: T. C. Newby, 1855. Vol. 1, frontispiece.

> Lady Blessington and Count D'Orsay presided at Gore House over one of the most gracious literary salons in London. She published a number of novels and other works, contributed to annuals, and edited the *Book of Beauty* from the volume for 1834. Landon contributed poems, and she and Landon were close friends.

57. *Old Gore House, in 1830.* "WP" [William Henry Prior], artist. Wood engraving in text, 4⅛ x 5⅝". In: *Old and New London,* vol. 5 (of 6), *The Western and Northern Suburbs.* London, Paris & New York: Cassell, Petter & Galpin [n.d., but 1887], p. 117.

> In Gore House, the large library, with two fireplaces, and with walls covered in books, was the *salle de réception,* as described by Mrs. Newton Crosland (Camilla Toulmin): "The furniture was delicate, apple-green silk damask set in white and gold, with fauteuils in abundance, . . . Summer and winter Lady Blessington always occupied the same seat, a large easy-chair near the fireplace, with a small table beside her, on which was probably a new book with the paper-knife between the leaves, and a scent-bottle and a fan" (pp. 101–102).

58. [L. E. L.] *Author of "Romance and Reality."* Daniel Maclise, artist. London: James Fraser [1833]. Reproduction of lithograph, 10⅝ x 8¼". In: *A Gallery of Illustrious Literary Characters.* Edited by William Bates. London: Chatto and Windus [n.d., but 1873]. Between pages 110 and 111. From lithograph originally published in *Fraser's Magazine,* vol. 8, no. 46 (October 1833), facing p. 433.

> Maclise's portraits for *Fraser's Magazine* present a vivid panorama of leading literary personalities of the 1830s. They were collected and republished with comments by William Bates, 1873 (quarto), and 1883 (8vo). See also Bates's article on the "Gallery" in *Notes and Queries* (March 11, 1871).

59. *Danl Maclise.* E. M. Ward, artist. J. Smyth, engraver. Reproduction of steel engraving, 10⅝ x 8¼". In: *A Gallery of Illustrious Literary Characters.* Edited by William Bates. London: Chatto and Windus [n.d., but 1873]. Facing page 228.

> Maclise grew up in Cork and came to London in 1827. When he won the gold medal of the Royal Academy in 1829 Landon wrote him a note saying that his success had given her "every pleasure but surprise" (Bates, p. 229). From 1830 he drew many portraits of Landon. Around 1835 rumor linked him with Landon.

60. *Jardin des Plantes.* T. Allom, artist. C. Heath, engraver. Steel engraving in text, 3½ x 4". In: Catherine Frances Gore, *Paris in 1841.* London: Longman, Brown, Green, and Longmans, 1842. Page 133. The volume has an alternate title on an additional engraved title-page: *Heath's Picturesque Annual for 1842: Paris.*

> Landon arrived in Paris on June 26, 1834 and on June 28 wrote to William Jerdan: "Who do you think I met on the Boulevards to-day? Mr. Gore" (*Letters,* p. 106). Letters from Paris are to William Jerdan unless otherwise noted.

61. *Catherine Frances Gore.* Artist unidentified. J. Freeman, engraver. London: Henry Colburn, 1837. Steel engraving, 8¾ x 5½". In: *The New Monthly Magazine,* vol. 49, no. 195 (March 1837), facing p. 305.

Catherine Gore (1799–1861) lived much of her life in Paris. In her professional career she published about 70 literary works, many of them three-decker novels of high quality.

62. *Revue des Deux Mondes,* vol. 6, no. 4 (May 15, 1832).

> This copy of an original issue of the *Revue des Deux Mondes* contains an article by Landon's friend Mme. Amable Tastu, "Une Jeune Poète anglaise," with a discussion of Landon, and translations, including a passage from *Romance and Reality.* About the editor of the *Revue,* François Buloz, Landon writes: "he has shown us the very greatest *civilité.* . . . He has given us a box for the opera next Wednesday" (*Letters,* p. 110).

63. *Paulina Duvernay, as the Maid of Terracina, in the Ballet called Il Briganti Performed at the King's Theatre in the Haymarket.* T. H. Jones, artist [n.p., n.d., but 1837]. Aquatint, 11 x 8⅜".

> In Paris, Landon saw the ballerina Pauline Duvernay dance "like an angel" (*Letters,* p. 115; correspondent unidentified). This print shows her in the "much admired Pas de Valse à la Tyrolienne," danced by her in ballet, *Le Brigand de Terracina,* adapted by Pilati (1837) from Auber's opera *Fra Diavolo, ou L'hôtellerie de Terracine* (1830).

64. *Boulevard des Italiens.* A. Hervieu, artist and etcher. London: Richard Bentley, 1835. Etching, 8⅜ x 5⅛". In: Frances Trollope, *Paris and the Parisians in 1835.* 2 vols. London: Richard Bentley, 1836. Illustration in vol. 2, facing p. 294.

> Landon wrote from Paris that Monsieur Buloz, editor of the *Revue des Deux Mondes,* "gave us a box at the opera the other night, where I was very much amused with the Tentation of Sainte Antoine. Then we went and had ices at Tortoni's—such a brilliant scene" (*Letters,* p. 114). Landon's rooms in the rue Taitbout were around the corner from the Café Tortoni.

65. *Antoine Fontaney.* Unsigned. Halftone, 7¾ x 4⅞". In: Antoine Fontaney, *Journal intime.* Edited by René Jasinski. Paris: Les Presses Françaises, 1925. Frontispiece. No. 6 of 300 numbered copies on *papier vergé d'Arches.*

> "The person whom I think the most interesting is a Monsieur Fontaney, a young poet of about four-and-twenty, or less. . . . He answers very well to my idea of a French genius—pale, dark, sombre, and with a sort of enthusiasm of which we have no idea in England" (*Letters,* p. 115; correspondent unidentified).

66. *Portrait of Heine* [unattributed; c. 1900?]. Steel engraving. 9⅞ x 6⅞". Individual print, derived from a sketch made in 1829 by Franz Kugler.

> Of Heine, Landon writes from Paris: "M. Heine called yesterday; a most pleasant person. I am afraid he did not think me a *personne bien spirituelle,* for you know it takes a long time with me to get over the shame of speaking to a stranger by way of conversation. He said, "Mademoiselle donc a beaucoup couru les boutiques?" "Mais non." "A-t-elle été au Jardin des Plantes?" "Mais non." "Avez vous été à l'opéra, aux théâtres?" "Mais non." Mademoiselle

aime la promenade?" "Mais non." "A-t-elle donc apporté beaucoup de livres, ou peut-être elle écrit?" "Mais non." At last, in seeming despair, he exclaimed, "Mais Mademoiselle, qu'est que ce donc, qu'elle a fait?" "Mais—mais—j'ai regardé par la fenêtre." Was there ever anything *si bête?* but I really could think of nothing else." She wrote later that Heine was "the wittiest and most original person" that she had seen in Paris (*Letters*, pp. 107–108; 118). An engraved version of this print by Eduard Mandel (1854) includes Heine's ms. inscription: "So sah ich aus, heute Morgen den 6ten April 1829 H. Heine" ("This is how I looked this morning, the 6th April 1829. H. Heine").

67. *Anecdotes.* Ape [Carlo Pellegrini], artist. [London:] Vincent Brooks Day & Son [1875]. Color lithograph, 15 x 10⅜". Individual print as published in: *Vanity Fair*, November 27, 1875.

> Abraham Hayward corresponded with Landon, and also with Heine, writing to introduce him to Landon. Hayward's English translation of Goethe's *Faust* was published in 1833.

68. Letitia Elizabeth Landon. Autograph letter signed, undated, to Abraham Hayward. Envelope with "A Hayward Esq" as addressee.

> Dear Mᵣ Hayward
> Instead of a formall call do let me persuade you to come to me on Thursday evening—pray do and more oblige
> > Your obliged
> > > L. E. Landon
> 22 Hans Place.

> The tiny envelope (2 x 2½") has a wax seal with the impression of Landon's script initials "L. E. L." within a rectangle with rounded corners.

69. *M. Odilon Barrot.* Wood engraving in text, 4¾ x 3". Individual print, as published in: *The Illustrated London News*, vol. 12, no. 304 (Saturday, February 26, 1848), p. 118.

> Odilon Barrot "is, you know, a most distinguished person; and, you do not know, has beautiful blue eyes. He went with us, yesterday, to the Pantheon; . . ." (*Letters*, p. 115; correspondent unidentified). Barrot was a prominent political figure and habitué of literary salons.

70. *Sainte-Beuve.* Carey, engraver. Paris: G. Havard [1855]. Steel engraving, 5⅜ x 3½". In: Eugène de Mirecourt, *Sainte-Beuve*. Paris: Gustave Havard, 1855. Frontispiece.

> Of Saint-Beuve, who later achieved the highest reputation for his literary criticism, Landon wrote from Paris: "I like Monsieur Sainte Beuve, he is very French, very animated, and, to use the national expression, *très-spirituelle*" (*Letters*, p. 109; spelling thus).

71. *P Mérimée.* Achille Devéria, artist. [New York: P. F. Collier & Son, 1901.] Heliogravure, 8 x 5¼". Individual print (derived from a unique lithographic proof executed c. 1828), as published in: Prosper Mérimée, *Colomba and Carmen,* translated by the Lady Mary Loyd. New York: P. F. Collier & Son, 1901. Frontispiece.

> "I have received so much kindness and attention from Monsieur Mérimée; he is very amusing, speaks English (a great fault in my eyes) like a native, and tells you all sorts of anecdotes in the most unscrupulous fashion" (*Letters,* p. 113). Mérimée's *Carmen* was published in 1845, and was the source for Bizet's opera (1875).

72. *1800.* Louis David, artist. Jules David, etcher. Paris: Victor-Havard, 1882. Etching, 10⅞ x 14⅛"; plate size, 5½ x 7¾"; image size, 4¾ x 7⅛". Individual etching, as published in: *Le Peintre Louis David 1748 1825: Suite d'eaux-fortes d'après ses œuvres gravées par J.-L. Jules David, son petit-fils.* Paris: Victor-Havard, 1882. Edition of 600 copies.

> This etching of David's well-known portrait of Madame Récamier was executed by the painter's grandson, Jules David, circa 1880 [pulled at the atelier of Alfred Salmon (1825–1894), later directed by Alfred Porcabeuf (b. 1867)]. Récamier's literary salon drew the most distinguished names in French literary and artistic circles. Landon wrote on July 19, 1834: "I am going to-day to Madame Récamier with Madame Tastu, to be presented to Chateaubriand" (*Letters,* p. 118). Jules David's work was a companion to his earlier volume *Le Peintre Louis David 1748–1825: Souvenirs & documents inédits* (Paris: Havard, 1880).

73. *Chateaubriand.* J. Gigoux, artist. Gustave Levy, engraver. Paris: Ernest Bourdin [1862]. Steel engraving, 10⅝ x 6⅜". Individual print, as published in: Jules Janin, *La Bretagne.* Paris: Ernest Bourdin, 1862. Frontispiece.

> Chateaubriand and Récamier were ardently devoted to one another, but never married. At her literary salons he would read chapters of his memoirs, which he did not want printed until after his death; hence the title, *Mémoires d'outre-tombe* ("Memoirs from beyond the grave").

74. *Lecture à l'Abbaye aux Bois.* A. Hervieu, artist and etcher. London: Richard Bentley, 1835. Etching, 8⅜ x 5⅛". In: Frances Trollope, *Paris and the Parisians in 1835.* 2 vols. London: Richard Bentley, 1836. Vol. 2, facing p. 228.

> Hervieu's rendering shows the very scene that Landon would have encountered at Mme. Récamier's apartment in l'Abbaye aux Bois. Over the mantelpiece is Gérard's dramatic painting of Mme. de Staël as Corinne at Cape Misena, a theme on which Landon published an impressive poem in *The Amulet* for 1832. Landon writes: "I was delighted with my visit to-day. Madame Récamier is really still beautiful, and with exquisite manners. I liked Chateaubriand so much." Here unfortunately she has to break off her letter—"I must not enter into details, for I have no time" (*Letters,* p. 118). In September 1836 she contributed to *The New Monthly Magazine* her essay "The Criticism of Chateaubriand."

75. *John Forster (1840).* Daniel Maclise, artist. Halftone, 8½ x 5¼″. In: Richard Renton, *John Forster and His Friendships.* London: Chapman and Hall, Ltd., 1912. Facing p. 58.

> Landon's engagement to the young journalist John Forster (b. 1812) seems to have begun around 1834, and was broken off in 1835 because of rumors circulating about her relationship with Jerdan, and apparently with others, such as William Maginn, and Daniel Maclise.

76. *L. E. L. / Letitia E. Landon.* D. McClise, artist. Finden, engraver. London: Saunders & Otley, 1835. Steel engraving, 6¾ x 4⅛″. In: *The Miscellaneous Poetical Works of L. E. L.,* Author of "The Improvisatrice," "The Golden Violet," &c. London: Saunders and Otley, 1835.

> Of this portrait, Landon's biographer Laman Blanchard commented that it "conveyed much" of the impression of her look and style of dress, as she might appear "some summer morning walking in the little garden of the house in Hans-place" (vol. 1, p. 144). However, the publisher Henry Vizetelly in his memoirs recalled: "... she was certainly most unattractive, and I failed to recognize any resemblance to the flattering portrait that formed the frontispiece to one of her books. The recollection I have preserved is of a pale-faced, plain-looking little woman, with lustreless eyes, and somewhat dowdily dressed, whom no amount of enthusiasm could have idealized into a sentimental poetess" (vol. 1, p. 127). *The Miscellaneous Poetical Works* was originally issued with the title *The Vow of the Peacock.*

77. *Giulia Grisi.* Rigo Frères, lithographers. Paris: Marchant [c. 1841–1842]. Lithograph on India paper, mounted, 9⅞ x 6⅛″. Individual print, as published in: *Galerie des Artistes-Dramatiques Composée de 80 Portraits et Notices.* Paris: Marchant [c. 1841–1842].

> Soon after Landon returned from Paris, she and Jerdan attended the opera, where they were visited in their box by Forster and Macready. One of the performers was Grisi, admired in Bellini's *Norma,* and in Donizetti's *Anna Bolena.* Landon wrote a poem on Grisi for Schloss's *Bijou Almanac* for 1838.

78. *Richard Bentley.* Lock & Whitfield, photographers. Joseph Brown, engraver. Steel engraving, 9¾ x 6″. In: *Richard Bentley & Son; Reprinted from 'Le Livre' of October 1885 with Some Additional Notes.* London: [N.p.], 1886.

> Richard Bentley and Henry Colburn published Landon's *Romance and Reality* in 1831. Bentley alone brought out *Francesca Carrara* in 1834. During the previous year Bentley had included in his Standard Novels series, Mme. de Staël's *Corinne,* translated by Isabel Hill, with poems in English versions by Landon. In 1848 he published in Standard Novels *Romance and Reality,* and reprinted the text in 1852.

79. *Regina's Maids of Honour.* Daniel Maclise, artist. Reproduction of lithograph, 10⅝ x 8¼″. In: *A Gallery of Illustrious Literary Characters.* Edited by William Bates. London: Chatto and Windus [n.d., but 1873]. Facing page 182. Originally published in *Fraser's Magazine*, vol. 13, no. 73 (January 1836).

> *Fraser's Magazine*, nicknamed "Regina," published work by leading women writers such as, from left, around the table: Anna Maria Hall (with glowing eyes); Landon (gesturing); Lady Morgan (back view); Caroline Norton (full face, with book); Lady Blessington (standing); Jane Porter (stirring coffee); Harriet Martineau (meditating); and Mary Russell Mitford (sipping coffee).

80. *Belsize House, Hampstead; View Looking North, 1812.* Digital photograph of an untitled original monochrome (sepia) wash drawing, 6 x 9″. Photograph by and reproduced with permission of Camden Local Studies and Archives Centre, London Borough of Camden.

> Matthew Forster was the senior partner in the firm of Forster and Smith, merchants in the Africa trade; also a Member of Parliament. Landon first met George Maclean at a party at Forster's house, Belsize House, Hampstead, in October 1836.

81. Letitia Elizabeth Landon. Autograph letter signed, to Mrs. Matthew Forster. Undated but with "Oct. 13ᵗʰ–1836" noted in pen at the bottom of the verso in a different hand:

> My dear Mrs Forster
>
> Many thanks for your kind invitation which I shall be delighted to accept. I return from Shirley Park early on Saturday—and shall, if you please, be ready for you by three o'clock. Will you pardon a hurried note for Mrs Skinner takes me down—and she is to go earlier than I expected.
>
> My kindest regards to your circle
> Your obliged and affectionate
> L. E. L.

> In October 1836 Landon was a guest at a dinner party at the home of Mr. and Mrs. Matthew Forster, Belsize House, Hampstead, when she first met George Maclean, whom she later married. It seems possible that this note may refer to that very party. On Shirley Park and Mrs. Skinner see cat. 54.

82. *Portrait of George Maclean.* Attributed to the circle of Stephen Pearce. Undated. Digital photograph of portrait at Westfield House, near Elgin, Scotland. Oil painting, 29 x 24″. Digital file provided by and reproduced with permission of John and Veronica Maclean.

Brodie Cruickshank, Maclean's right-hand man in Africa, and author of a memoir titled *Eighteen Years on the Gold Coast* (1853), records Landon's account of her first meeting, in October 1836, with George Maclean. She had imagined him as "some grey-haired officer with a mixture of sternness and benevolence in his countenance." At the dinner party, "Mr. Maclean was the last to enter the dining-room, and great was her surprise to see, what she was pleased to call, 'a very fine and fashionable looking man in the prime of life'" (vol. 1, p. 216).

83. *L. E. Landon.* J. Wright, artist. S. Freeman, engraver. London: Henry Colburn, 1837. Steel engraving, 8¾ x 5½″. In: *The New Monthly Magazine*, vol. 50, no. 197 (May 1837). Frontispiece.

> Of Wright's portrait, Anna Maria Hall commented: "a very poor affair it was, giving one the idea of a pert chambermaid rather than the authoress of the 'Improvisatrice'" (pp. 3–4).

84. *W. C. Macready.* R. Thorburn, artist. C. H. Jeens, engraver. London: Macmillan & Co., 1875. Steel engraving, 7⅜ x 4½″. Individual print, as published in: *Macready's Reminiscences, and Selections from His Diaries and Letters.* Edited by Sir Frederick Pollock. New York: Macmillan and Co., 1875. Facing p. 531.

> William Charles Macready, a leading actor, was theater-manager at Covent Garden. Landon wanted to submit her tragedy *Castruccio Castrucani* for possible performance in the spring of 1838, but by the time she had the manuscript ready, the schedule was filled up.

85. *Theatre Royal, Covent Garden.* Thos. H. Shepherd, artist. John Rolph, engraver. London: Jones & Co., 1828. Steel engraving, 5⅜ x 8⅛″. Individual print, as published in: Thomas H. Shepherd, *Metropolitan Improvements.* London: Jones & Co., 1827–1828.

> As manager of the Theatre Royal, Covent Garden, Macready presented, among other plays in spring 1838, Bulwer's *The Lady of Lyons*, with Helena Faucit in the role of Pauline, the "Lady of Lyons," and himself as her lover, Claude Melnotte.

86. *Pauline in the Lady of Lyons from a painting by Miss Myra Drummond.* Walker & Cockerell, photographers and engravers. Photogravure, 8½ x 5½″. In: Sir Theodore Martin, *Helena Faucit (Lady Martin).* Edinburgh and London: William Blackwood and Sons, 1900. Facing p. 50.

> Landon wrote to Bulwer about his play: "On Thursday last I saw the Lady of Lyons—much as I was delighted when I read it I was still more delighted to see it— It was a succession of exquisite pictures—" (*Biography*, p. 301).

87. *The English Bijou Almanac for 1838.* Poetically illustrated by L. E. L. London: Schloss [published late 1837].

> Albert Schloss's *Bijou Almanac* was a tour de force of book production. The book measures about ¾ by ½ of an inch, with 64 pages. Each issue usually included six short poems about

celebrated personalities, including opera divas Giulia Grisi (cat. 77), Maria Malibran, and Giuditta Pasta.

88. *Arabia.* Fanny Corbaux, artist. E. Finden, engraver. London: J. Hogarth, 1850. Hand-colored steel engraving, 14 x 10″. In: *Findens' Tableaux of National Character, Beauty, and Costume.* 2 vols. London: J. Hogarth [n.d., but 1850]. Landon's poem "The Arab Maid," on pp. 8–9 of vol. 1, with plate facing p. 8.

> In the late 1830s publishers were bringing out ever more elaborate annuals. *Finden's Tableaux* began in 1836 (volume for 1837), and continued through 1843 (for 1844). This edition comprises the contents of the five volumes published for 1837 through 1841. Landon's contribution appeared in the first volume (for 1837).

89. *Water Lilies.* Fanny Corbaux, artist. G. Adcock, engraver. London: Ackermann & Co., 1837. Steel engraving, 13¼ x 10⅜″. In: *Flowers of Loveliness; Twelve Groups of Female Figures, Emblematic of Flowers.* Poetical illustrations by L. E. L. London: Ackermann and Company, 1838. With poem "The Water-Lily."

> Flowers illustrated in these emblematic scenes are: Clematis, Hyacinth, Heath, Water-Lily, Night-Blowing Convolvulus, Poppy, Canterbury Bell, Pansy, Marvel of Peru, Laurel, Iris, and Mignonette. Artists: Fanny Corbaux (4 prints), Joseph Kenny Meadows (3 prints), Louise Seyffarth (1 print), Eliza Sharpe (1 print), Thomas Uwins (3 prints).

90. *The Honble. Frances Diana Manners Sutton, Daughter of Viscount Canterbury.* J. Bostock, artist. H. Robinson, engraver. London: Longman & Co., 1837. Steel engraving, 13⅝ x 10½″. In: *Portraits of the Children of the Nobility.* Edited by Mrs. [Louisa] Fairlie. First Series. London: Longman, Orme, Brown, Green, and Longmans, 1838.

> This volume contains Landon's poem "The Portrait of the Hon. Frances Diana Manners Sutton, Daughter of Viscount Canterbury."

91. *L. E. Landon.* Daniel Maclise, artist. New York: Johnson, Wilson & Co. [1873]. Steel engraving, 10⅞ x 8⅛″. Individual print, as published in: Evert A. Duyckinck, *Portrait Gallery of Eminent Men and Women of Europe and America.* 2 vols. New York: Johnson, Wilson & Company, 1873. Vol. 2, facing p. 244.

> Maclise's well-known portrait of Landon was issued in many versions. His original pencil drawing (National Portrait Gallery, London) shows a sparkle in the expression, while the engravings are more iconic. See also cat. 99.

92. No. 43 Connaught Street, London. Digital photograph by Margaret Baker, 2009.

> In February 1837 Landon moved from 22 Hans Place to this Georgian town house, built circa 1828 as No. 28 Upper Berkeley Street West. Before 1879 the street name was changed and houses renumbered. No. 43 Connaught Street seems to be the only one of Landon's London residences that remains standing.

93. *St. Mary's Church, Wyndham Place, & District Rectory to St. Mary-le-Bone.* Thos. H. Shepherd, artist. Archer, engraver. London: Jones & Co., 1828. Steel engraving, 7⅞ x 5″. Individual print, as published in: Thomas H. Shepherd, *Metropolitan Improvements.* London: Jones & Co., 1827–1828.

> Letitia Elizabeth Landon and George Maclean were married on June 7, 1838 at St. Mary's Church, Bryanston Square. Landon's brother, the Reverend Whittington Henry Landon, officiated; Bulwer gave away the bride. Witnesses who signed the record were Bulwer, and Landon's cousin Mary Elizabeth Landon, from Aberford.

94. *Crockford's Club House, St. James's Street.* Tho. H. Shepherd, artist. Wm. Tombleson, engraver. London: Jones & Co., 1828. Steel engraving, 5¾ x 8⅛″. Individual print, as published in: Thomas H. Shepherd, *Metropolitan Improvements.* London: Jones & Co., 1827–1828.

> Victoria acceded to the throne on June 20, 1837. Her coronation took place on Thursday, June 28, 1838. Landon watched the procession from windows at Crockford's Club, 50 St. James's Street.

95. *Optogt ter Krooning van Koningin Victoria* ["Procession at the Coronation of Queen Victoria"]. Steendr. van H. J. Backer ["Lithograph by H. J. Backer," 1838]. Colored lithograph, 4⅝ x 8″. Individual print, as published in: *Het Leeskabinet: Mengelwerk tot Gezellig onderhoud voor beschaafde kringen voor 1838* ["The Reading Room: Miscellany for Pleasant Entertainment for Cultivated Circles for 1838"]. Derde deel, met platen ["Part 3, with plates"]. Amsterdam: Hendrik Frijlink, 1838. Facing p. 264.

> As Landon viewed the coronation procession from Crockford's Club, June 28, 1838, she "wore"—as Katherine Thomson recalled—"a white bridal bonnet and a simple muslin dress, and with a party of friends stood in a balcony, waving her handkerchief in the enthusiasm of the moment as the troops appeared. As the last regiment of the gorgeous Lancers rode down the street she suddenly withdrew, and those who were watching her from the opposite window saw her no more" (p. 190).

96. *Plate of the Brig "Governor Maclean."* W. J. Huggins, artist. C. Rosenberg, engraver. London: W. J. Huggins [c. 1833]. Digital photograph by, and reproduced with permission, © National Maritime Museum, Greenwich, London. Dimensions of original aquatint, 15⅛ x 21⅝″.

> Landon and Maclean embarked on Tuesday, July 3, 1838. As the brig *Governor Maclean* sailed toward the Gulf of Guinea, Landon kept a journal, noting, for example: "The only light is that in the binnacle, where the compass is placed, by which the course is steered; it is such a speck of light for the safety of the whole to depend upon.... Friday, August 10. We can now see the land...." (*Letters,* p. 185.) The *Governor Maclean* continued in service until

September 5, 1864 when it was wrecked "on the Owers Sandbank, off Selsey," according to a notice in *The Life-Boat* (January 1, 1865).

97. *The Castle in Which "L. E. L." Died.* Wood engraving in text, 3¼ x 4½". In: *The Mirror of Literature, Amusement, and Instruction*, vol. 33, no. 933 (Saturday, January 26, 1839), p. 49. An original issue of the journal.

Contemporary renderings tend to show Cape Coast Castle as more grandiose than it really was. A central stairway leads up to main hall, and to the left (seaward) were the rooms Maclean and Landon occupied. She died suddenly on the morning of October 15, 1838; the official verdict was that her death "was caused by her having incautiously taken an overdose of prussic acid, which, from evidence, it appeared she had been in the habit of using as a remedy for spasmodic affections to which she was subject." In medical terminology of the period, "affections" refers to "conditions" or "complaints." The verdict of the inquest was published in *The Times* (London), January 4, 1839 (p. 6).

98. *The Grave of "L. E. L." in Cape Coast Castle.* Wood engraving in text, 8⅞ x 4"; page size, 15⅝ x 11⅜". Individual page from *The Graphic* (London), August 8, 1873, p. 121.

Brodie Cruickshank oversaw the burial: "Night had come on before the paving-stones were all put down over the grave, and the workmen finished their business by torchlight" (vol. 1, p. 229). Of Maclean's death in 1847 Charles Alexander Gordon recorded: "Her husband, Captain George Maclean, died under my care, his body was laid beside hers, the coffins touching each other; . . . ." Of Landon he writes: ". . . she died suddenly, her death, I feel quite satisfied, having been occasioned by heart disease, of which for a considerable time she had been the subject" (p. 56). Gordon (1821–1899) served as a medical officer at Cape Coast Castle in 1847–1848.

99. *Fisher's Drawing Room Scrap-Book.* MDCCCXL. With poetical illustrations by L. E. L. and Mary Howitt. London and Paris: Fisher, Son, & Co. [published late 1839]. With memorial frontispiece of Landon by Maclise.

From Africa, Landon was planning to edit the *Drawing Room Scrap Book* for 1840, but she died before she could complete it. There are five poems by her. The front cover stamping shows a classical urn, suggestive of mourning; the back cover shows allegorical figures of poetry (lyre) joined with art (palette), as in the contents. The frontispiece, from Maclise's portrait (cat. 91), has a facsimile signature ("L. E. L. / Cape Coast Castle October 12") and three lines from Landon's poem "Shuhur, Jeypore" (1833) engraved in script lettering:

> Alas! hope is not prophecy,—we dream,
> But rarely does the glad fulfillment come:
> We leave our land—and we return no more!

100. L. E. Landon. *Poetical Works of Letitia Elizabeth Landon.* 2 vols. London: Longman, Brown, Green, and Longmans, 1850. The title-page vignette is a scene from *The Troubadour.* "RD" [Richard Doyle], artist. I. A. Thomson, engraver.

> This edition includes the contents of the previous four-volume edition (1829, 1839, 1844), *The Improvisatrice, The Troubadour, The Golden Violet,* and *The Venetian Bracelet,* as rearranged for publication in two volumes. Printings were issued in 1850, 1853, 1855, 1860, 1863 (dated 1864), and 1867, and the edition remained in print until at least 1870. These volumes are usually found in leather bindings. This is the only set I have seen in the original cloth binding as issued.

101. *Tintagel.* William Bell Scott, artist. Dalziel, engraver. Wood engraving, 7⅛ x 4⅞". In: *The Poetical Works of Letitia Elizabeth Landon (L. E. L.),* edited by William B. Scott. London and New York: George Routledge and Sons [n.d., but 1884]. In the series "Routledge's Red-Line Poets." Illustration facing p. 495, for Landon's "A Legend of Tintagel Castle."

> William Bell Scott, a friend of Rossetti and Swinburne, shows strong Pre-Raphaelite influences in his illustrations for Landon's poems. Scott's collection was first published by Routledge in 1873, with further editions in 1880 and 1884 (all undated), continuing in print until the 1890s. *The Poetical Works* was reprinted in 1990.

NOTES

1. "The History of a Child," in Landon's *Traits and Trials of Early Life* (London: Henry Colburn, 1836; reprint edition, Ann Arbor, Michigan: Scholars' Facsimiles & Reprints [hereafter, "SF&R"], 1999), p. 312.

2. A number of more or less fictional works have been written about Landon: Louise von Ploennies, "Die Sappho des Westens," in *Neue Gedichte* (Darmstadt: G. Jonghaus, 1851)—this author also published in her anthology titled *Britannia* (Frankfurt a.M.: Schmerber, 1843) German translations of poems by Landon; Anna Maria Hall, *A Woman's Story*, 3 vols. (London: Hurst & Blackett, 1857); D. E. Enfield, *L. E. L.: A Mystery of the Thirties* (London: Hogarth Press, 1928); "Joseph Shearing" (Margaret Vere Campbell), *The Golden Violet* (New York: Smith & Durrell, 1941); Helen Ashton, *Letty Landon* (London and New York: Dodd, Mead & Company, 1951); Clyde Chantler, *Eight Weeks: A Novel* (London: Linden Press, 1965); Michael Gorman, *L. E. L.: The Life and Murder of Letitia E. Landon: A Flower of Loveliness* (London: Olympia Publishers, 2008).

3. Landon's birth date is recorded in the parish register as part of her baptismal entry. Though this would normally be considered definitive evidence for the date, puzzling inconsistencies remain. See discussion in: F. J. Sypher, *Letitia Elizabeth Landon: A Biography*, 2nd edition, revised (SF&R, 2009; 1st edition, 2004), pp. 11–13 and notes; also pp. 176–177, and notes on pp. 371, 386, 400.

4. No documentary references have so far been found to verify details of his career at sea, as mentioned by Blanchard and other memoirists.

5. It has been suggested that Mrs. Bishop may have been "the natural daughter of an aristocratic family"; William Jerdan, *The Autobiography of William Jerdan*, 4 vols. (London: Arthur Hall, Virtue & Co., 1852–1853), vol. 3 (1853), p. 180. Searches in public records have brought to light surprisingly few traces of the activities of Landon's mother and father (and no portraits of them have been located).

6. Landon mentions her birthplace in an unpublished letter to Anna Maria Hall (undated but evidently 1837; Princeton University Library, Department of Rare Books and Special Collections). Biographical sketch in *The Book of Gems* for 1838 (published late 1837)—"born in Hans Place"; see *Biography*, p. 353, note 10; and *Letters*, edited by F. J. Sypher (SF&R, 2001), pp. 167–168.

7. Jerdan, *Autobiography*, vol. 3 (1853), p. 174.

8. *The Morning Chronicle*, Wednesday, July 26, 1820, p. 4. See *Biography*, pp. 39–40, and notes on pp. 363–364.

9. "*Romance and Reality* by L. E. L.," *The New Monthly Magazine*, vol. 32 (new series), no. 132 (December 1831), pp. 545–551; quotation from pp. 546–547. Attribution to Bulwer by Michael

Sadleir in *Bulwer: A Panorama, I, Edward and Rosina 1803-1836* (Boston: Little, Brown, and Company, 1931), pp. 390–394.

10. *The Literary Gazette*, no. 264 (Saturday, February 9, 1822), p. 89.

11. See *Biography,* "Appendix 3, Musical Settings," pp. 324–345.

12. *The Literary Gazette,* no. 389 (Saturday, July 3, 1824), pp. 417–420.

13. John Landon may have become subject to a sheriff's execution to seize his property in order to pay creditors. It is conceivable that he may have been confined for debt, as in King's Bench Prison; or perhaps he may have been prosecuted for theft or embezzlement. Or he could have fled to France or elsewhere to avoid imprisonment or prosecution. A London document researcher whom I consulted about these suggestions indicated that the voluminous relevant records would have to be examined case by case.

14. Copy at Yale University, Beinecke Rare Book and Manuscript Library, Speck Collection.

15. From "Archibald Constable and His Literary Friends," *Chambers's Journal,* 6th series, vol. 5, nos. 257–258 (November 1, 1902; November 8, 1902), pp. 755–758, 780–783. By November 7, 1825 Milliken was at Lasswade, having left Landon at Aberford the evening of the 5th. The diarist is not named by the anonymous editor, but from details given in the article, and from *Archibald Constable and His Literary Correspondents: A Memorial,* edited by Thomas Constable, 3 vols. (Edinburgh: Edmonston and Douglas, 1873), and other sources, the diarist can be identified as Richard Milliken of Dublin, later vicar of Stoughton, who died May 13, 1863; death notice in the *Gentleman's Magazine,* June 1863, p. 802. "Wolfe's Remains" refers to: *Remains of the Rev. Charles Wolfe,* edited by John A. Russell (Dublin: A. and W. Watson, 1825), including "The Burial of Sir John Moore after Corunna." Related letters, unpublished, are at the National Library of Scotland: Jerdan to Constable, Landon to Constable; and draft of Constable's letter to Landon. Landon's statement that she "never went to school" fits with her comment in *The Book of Gems* that her childhood was passed at Trevor Park, and is inconsistent with memoirists' accounts of her attending Miss Rowden's school at Hans Place. Elsewhere she states, as here, that she is an "orphan." Some memoirists comment that Landon was not always truthful in her statements; on the other hand, it is apparent that her memoirists do not always give accurate information either, so it is sometimes difficult to know what to accept.

16. Letter by Frances Trollope to Mary Russell Mitford, April 22, 1827, in *The Friendships of Mary Russell Mitford as Recorded in Letters from Her Literary Correspondents,* edited by the Rev. A. G. L'Estrange (New York: Harper & Brothers, 1882), p. 123. Discussion in *Bibliography,* p. 188.

17. "Memoir," with *Romance and Reality* (London: Richard Bentley, 1848), p. xix (anonymous, but internal evidence shows Jerdan's authorship); see also *The Autobiography of William Jerdan,* vol. 3, pp. 170–171. No love letters or journals are known that might provide a first-hand basis for understanding their relationship. Landon's known letters to Jerdan (with the exception of letters from Paris) cover mainly routine business matters relating to the *Gazette.*

18. "Sapphics and Erotics," *The Sunday Times*, March 5, 1826, p. [3]. First discussed by Cynthia Lawford in her article " 'Thou shalt bid thy fair hands rove': L. E. L.'s Wooing of Sex, Pain, Death, and the Editor," in *Érudit, Romanticism on the Net*, no. 29–30 (February–May 2003).

19. Article in *The Wasp*, October 7, 1826. First discussed by Germaine Greer in "The Tulsa Center for the Study of Women's Literature: What We Are Doing and Why We Are Doing It," *Tulsa Studies in Women's Literature*, vol. 1, no. 1 (Spring 1982), pp. 5–26.

20. Letter by James T. B. Landon in *The Pall Mall Gazette*, no. 340 (Monday, March 12, 1866), p. 811. See *Biography*, pp. 173, 398 note 62.

21. Word "criminalities" in *The Queens of Society*, by Katherine Thomson with her son John C. Thomson (as "Grace and Philip Wharton"), 3rd edition (London and New York: George Routledge and Sons, 1867; 1st edition, 1860), p. 183. Katherine Byerley (1797–1862) in 1820 married Anthony Todd Thomson (1778–1849), Landon's personal physician for many years, apparently from her infancy.

22. Articles by Cynthia Lawford, as cited in *Biography*, p. 449, especially "Diary," *The London Review of Books*, vol. 22, no. 18 (September 21, 2000), pp. 36–37; and " 'Thou shalt bid thy fair hands rove' . . ." cited above, note 18.

23. Unpublished letter to Francis Mahony, December 1834, National Library of Scotland, MS. 3219, folios 34–35.

24. *Magazin für die Literatur des Auslandes*, vol. 1, no. 124 (Monday, November 12, 1832), p. 494.

25. Jewsbury in *The Athenaeum*, no. 214 (Saturday, December 10, 1831), pp. 793–795. Attribution of this anonymous review in: Monica Correa Fryckstedt, "The Hidden Rill: The Life and Career of Maria Jane Jewsbury: II," *Bulletin of the John Rylands Library*, vol. 67, no. 1 (Autumn 1974), p. 473. On Bulwer's review, see above, note 9.

26. James Blackwood edition in boards advertised in *The Athenaeum*, November 12, 1859. See: Chester W. Topp, *Victorian Yellowbacks & Paperbacks, 1849–1905*, 9 vols. (Denver, Colorado: Hermitage Antiquarian Bookshop, 1993–2009), vol. 2 (1995), p. 385. On other Landon editions listed by Topp: vol. 1, p. 133; vol. 2, p. 15. See advertisements in *The Athenaeum*, no. 1585 (March 13, 1858), p. 323 (auction); nos. 1672, 1677 (November 12; December 17, 1859), pp. 620, 801 (Blackwood); no. 2283 (July 29, 1871), p. 144 (Blackwood, 5s. edition).

27. *The Literary Gazette*, no. 1128 (Saturday, September 1, 1838), p. 556; see *Biography*, p. 412 for discussion of attribution to Mme. de Gaudrion.

28. Letter to Mary Anne Wyndham Lewis, week of October 14, 1833, in *Letters* (SF&R, 2001), p. 94.

29. Manuscript at University of Iowa Libraries; discussion and text in *Critical Writings* (SF&R, 1996), pp. 88–91, and 169–170.

30. Profile of Bulwer attributed to Landon by S. C. Hall, *Retrospect of a Long Life: from 1815 to 1883*, 2 vols. (London: Richard Bentley & Son, 1883), vol. 1, p. 273.

31. Letters by Landon from Paris are in *Letters* (SF&R, 2001); Duvernay, p. 115; Tortoni's, p. 114; see *Biography*, p. 151.

32. Quotation: "nobody" in town; *Letters*, p. 108; *Biography*, p. 149.

33. Mme. Tastu published other French translations of work by Landon, as listed in *Bibliography*, p. 123. She also included a poem by Landon, headed "Le Cyprès" (with text in English; "The Cypress," from *The Amulet* for 1826), in a French anthology: *La Couronne de Flore, ou mélange de poésie et de prose* par Mesdames Desbordes-Valmore, Amable Tastu, la comtesse de Bradi, et M. Jules Baget; Ce receuil est destiné à accompagner *la Naissance des Fleurs*, ouvrage lithographique composé de 300 groupes de fleurs, par MM. Redouté, Baget, Dumas, etc. (Paris: Fleury Chavant, Éditeur, 1837).

34. On Fontaney, see *Letters*, p. 113; also 115, 118; *Biography*, p. 149.

35. On Récamier, see *Letters*, p. 118; *Biography*, p. 151.

36. On "rumours and stories," see *The Diaries of William Charles Macready 1833-1851*, edited by William Toynbee, 2 vols. (New York: G. P. Putnam's Sons, 1912), vol. 1, p. 262.

37. Forster as "imperious and overbearing"; letter to Bulwer, *Biography*, p. 291.

38. Berkeley and Maginn; *Biography*, pp. 168–173.

39. For Landon's translations from German see *Poems from the Literary Gazette* (SF&R, 2003), and notes, pp. 528–529. At the time the notes were written for that volume, the source was untraced for "Pauline's Price" (attributed by Landon to Goethe); it is not from Goethe, but from Bürger's "Mollys Wert" ("Ach, könnt' ich Molly kaufen"). Also, the poem from Herder rendered as "Whither would ye draw me, fair and faithless eyes" is "Das Meer der Liebe" ("Wohin ziehest du mich, du sanft hinschwimmendes Auge?"). On Jerdan's efforts as a literary agent for her, see: Harry Ransom, "William Jerdan, Editor and Literary Agent," *Studies in English*, vol. 27, no. 1 (June 1948), pp. 68–74. Jerdan's correspondence with Bentley about Landon, and others, is at the Harry Ransom Center of the University of Texas at Austin.

40. Details on Jerdan in *Poems from The New Monthly Magazine* (SF&R, 2007), pp. 127–131.

41. Bennoch's comments: in Hawthorne, *The English Notebooks 1853-1856*, edited by Thomas Woodson, and Bill Ellis, in *The Centenary Edition of the Works of Nathaniel Hawthorne*, vol. 21 (Ohio State University Press, 1997), p. 424; see also *Poems from the New Monthly Magazine* (SF&R, 2007), pp. 127–131.

42. On Landon's autobiographical sketch for *The Book of Gems*, see *Letters* (SF&R, 2001), pp. 167–168.

43. Mary Shenai, *Finding the Bergheims of Belsize Court* (London: Belsize Conservation Area

Advisory Committee, 2007) contains reproductions of photographs from the early 1900s, when the house was still standing (renamed Belsize Court; demolished 1937). Interior photos show the very rooms, as later redecorated, where Landon and Maclean met. See also *The Streets of Belsize: A Survey of Streets, Houses and Residents in the Southern Sector of Hampstead . . .* , edited by Christopher Wade (London: Camden History Society, 1991), pp. 76–77.

44. Brodie Cruickshank, *Eighteen Years on the Gold Coast of Africa*, 2nd edition, with new introduction by A. K. Busia, 2 vols. (London: Frank Cass; New York: Barnes & Noble, 1966; reprint of London edition of 1853), vol. 1, p. 216.

45. Landon in a letter of March 1838 to Bulwer writes about seeing *The Lady of Lyons;* see *Biography*, p. 301.

46. Judging from the diary quoted above (note 15), the carriage seems to have gone from London to Aberford in two or three days, including November 4–5, and from Aberford to Lasswade in two days, November 6–7. If Maclean and Landon were traveling by private carriage, they may have been able to include the wedding. Time by private carriage would have been considerably faster than by coach. The brides-to-be were Landon's cousins Lucy Landon (marrying George Henry Whitaker), and Dorothy Snell Landon (marrying Francis Watt), both on Saturday, June 19, 1838. See *Poems from the New Monthly Magazine* (SF&R, 2007), p. 124.

47. This explanation is given by Jaime Cortesão, in *Os Descobrimentos Portugueses*, 3 vols. (*Obras completas*, vols. 21–23), vol. 3 (Lisbon: Livros Horizonte, 1975), pp. 677–678; see *Biography*, p. 401.

48. Brodie Cruickshank, *Eighteen Years on the Gold Coast*, vol. 1, p. 222.

49. *Biography*, p. 424, note 33, lists sources on prussic acid in Landon's day. To these may be added: Edward John Waring, *Bibliotheca Therapeutica, or Bibliography of Therapeutics, Chiefly in Reference to Articles of the Materia Medica*, 2 vols., Publications of the New Sydenham Society, vols. 78 and 82 (London: The New Sydenham Society, 1878–1879), vol. 2 (1879), pp. 506–510.

50. Emma Roberts, who had known Landon "intimately from the first period of her girlhood," expresses the opinion—especially in light of Landon's "perfect happiness" in her marriage—that her death was "wholly accidental." Note also, in reference to Landon's recollection of her early years (see above, note 15), Roberts's statement that the Landon family moved from Chelsea to Trevor Park when Landon "was yet an infant," and there she "spent the days of her early childhood" (no mention of attendance at school in London). Quotations from pp. 6–7, and 31–32 of "Memoir" in *The Zenana*, cited in bibliography.

51. This collection began with the purchase of a copy of volume 1 (only) of the 1850 printing, plucked from the shelves of the long-gone Abbey Book Shop, 61 Fourth Avenue, by Peggy Kirby on a brilliant sunny summer day when we were together browsing there, June 30, 1987, πάλαι ποτά ("long ago").

52. Routledge's New York office was on Lafayette Place, a quiet, tree-lined, fashionable residential street from its opening in 1826, when nearby Great Jones Street and Bond Street were sought-after addresses; see "23 Bond Street: The Story of a House Where Time Stood Still," *Social Register Observer*, no. 28 (November 2007), pp. 22–26. Later many of the houses were taken over for commercial purposes. No. 9 Lafayette Place, where Routledge remained from early 1881 until April 1895 (as seen in advertisements in *Publishers' Weekly*), was on the west side of the street, between Great Jones Street and Fourth Street. After 1886 Lafayette Place gradually became Lafayette Street, as it is known today, with a revised system of house numbers. Scott's edition was also issued with the imprint: Boston: Lee and Shepard; New York: Lee, Shepard, and Dillingham, 1874 (published late 1873).

BIBLIOGRAPHY

FOR A DETAILED account of Landon's publications see: F. J. Sypher, *Letitia Elizabeth Landon: A Bibliography* (Ann Arbor, Michigan: Scholars' Facsimiles & Reprints, 2005); also *Letitia Elizabeth Landon: A Biography*, 2nd edition (SF&R, 2009; 1st edition, 2004). SF&R has published about 17 volumes of scholarly editions of Landon's poems, novels, short stories, criticism, letters, and other works, including several collections containing material not reprinted elsewhere: *Poems from The New Monthly Magazine* (2007); *Poems from Annuals* (2006); *Poems from The Literary Gazette* (2003); *Castruccio Castrucani* (2000); *Letters* (1999); *Tales and Sketches* (1999); and *Critical Writings* (1996).

There is no known major collection of Landon's papers. Manuscripts are widely scattered among institutional libraries and private collections. The whereabouts of important materials that as of 1841 were available to Landon's literary executor and biographer, Laman Blanchard, are presently unknown. A desirable aid to future research would be a comprehensive catalogue, with locations, of Landon's letters and other manuscripts.

Aside from SF&R publications, works cited in the catalogue in abbreviated form are listed below with the catalogue number where the work is mentioned.

Bates, William. *Notes and Queries*, series 4, vol. 7, no. 167 (March 11, 1871), pp. 211–214. Cat. 58.

Blanchard, Laman. *Life and Literary Remains of L. E. L.* 2 vols. London: Henry Colburn, 1841. Cat. 76.

Cass, F. C. *East Barnet.* Westminster: London and Middlesex Archæological Society, 1885–1892. Cat. 8.

Crosland, Mrs. Newton (Camilla Toulmin). *Landmarks of a Literary Life 1820–1892.* London: Sampson Low, Marston & Company, 1893. Cat. 57.

Cruickshank, Brodie. *Eighteen Years on the Gold Coast of Africa.* Introduction by K. A. Busia. 2nd edition. 2 vols. London: Frank Cass & Co. Ltd.; New York: Barnes & Noble, Inc., 1966; 1st edition, London, 1853. Cat. 82, 98.

Gordon, Charles Alexander. *Life on the Gold Coast.* London etc.: Baillière, Tindall & Cox, et al., 1874. Cat. 98.

Hall, S. C., and Anna Maria. "The Portraits of L. E. L." *The Art-Union* [later *The Art Journal*], vol. 1, no. 1 (February 15, 1839), pp. 3–4. Cat. 29, 83.

Life-Boat, The, or Journal of the National Life-Boat Institution, vol. 5, no. 55 (January 1, 1865), p. 551. Cat. 96.

Lytton, Rosina Bulwer Lytton, Lady [*née* Rosina Wheeler]. *Unpublished Letters of Lady Bulwer Lytton to A. E. Chalon, R.A.* Edited by S. M. Ellis. London: Eveleigh Nash, 1914. Cat. 34.

Pickford, John. *Notes and Queries,* series 5, vol. 10, no. 236 (July 6, 1878), pp. 18–19. Cat. 3.

Roberts, Emma. "Memoir of L. E. L." In: L. E. Landon. *The Zenana and Minor Poems.* London and Paris: Fisher, Son, & Co. [1839]. Cat. 8.

Thomson, Katherine, with John C. Thomson (writing as "Grace and Philip Wharton"). *The Queens of Society.* 3rd edition. London and New York: George Routledge and Sons, 1867. Cat. 95.

Vizetelly, Henry. *Glances Back through Seventy Years: Autobiographical and Other Reminiscences.* 2 vols. London: Kegan Paul, Trench, Trübner & Co., Ltd., 1893. Cat. 76.

━━━━━━━━━

INDEX

References are to page numbers, unless preceded by "cat." indicating catalogue items.
An italic number indicates a page with relevant illustration(s).

Index

Index

*Two hundred copies printed
from Miller & Bulmer types on Mohawk paper.
Design and typography by
Jerry Kelly.*